COLD SHOT
TO THE
HEART

ALSO BY WALLACE STROBY

Gone 'til November
The Heartbreak Lounge
The Barbed-Wire Kiss

COLD SHOT
TO THE
HEART

Wallace Stroby

Minotaur Books

New York

COLD SHOT TO THE HEART. Copyright © 2011 by Wallace Stroby. All rights reserved. Printed in the United States of America. For information, address St. Martin's Press, 175 Fifth Avenue, New York, N.Y. 10010.

www.minotaurbooks.com

Library of Congress Cataloging-in-Publication Data

Stroby, Wallace.
    Cold shot to the heart / Wallace Stroby.—1st ed.
      p. cm.
    ISBN 978-0-312-56025-6
    1. Female offenders—Fiction.   2. Card games—Fiction.   3. Ex-convicts—Fiction. I. Title.
    PS3619.T755C65 2011
    813'.6—dc22

2010037538

First Edition: January 2011

10 9 8 7 6 5 4 3 2 1

There is no such thing as moral phenomena, but only a moral interpretation of phenomena.

—Friedrich Nietzsche,
Beyond Good and Evil

Keep in mind, kid, until your dying day, the only crime anywhere in the world is being broke.

—"Oklahoma" Smith,
as quoted by John Seybold

COLD SHOT
TO THE
HEART

ONE

Three minutes after she walked in the front door, Crissa had the manager and two clerks facedown on the floor, their hands bound behind them with plastic cuffs.

She took away their guns—snub-noses in belt clip holsters— and dumped them in the flip-top trash can against the wall. All three had been wearing their guns openly, but they hadn't gone for them. She'd drawn the Glock, come around the counter fast, gesturing at the floor, and they'd knelt without protest, hands behind their heads. They knew the drill, valued their lives more than the money.

She put the Glock away, went back and locked the front door. Rain slanted out of the gray sky, ran down the plate-glass window. Only 4:00 P.M., but nearly night already. They'd turned on the neon sign that read CHECK CASHING MONEY TRANSFERS PAY DAY LOANS. She hit a wall switch and the sign buzzed, went dark. She flipped the old-fashioned door placard to CLOSED.

When she crossed behind the counter again, the men hadn't moved. All three were Latinos, one older and grayer, the manager. They were lying still, waiting it out.

She went through a door into the back room—desk, filing cabinets, a big green Honeywell safe. The safe door was ajar, as expected. She found the breaker box on the wall, clicked everything to OFF. The office lights blinked out; the computer on the desk hummed and died.

At the metal fire door, she listened, heard the sound of an engine outside in the alley. She rapped twice with gloved knuckles. After a moment, there came an answering knock from outside. She set her hand on the panic bar, paused. If the rear door alarm was connected to a separate breaker box— one she hadn't found—they were in trouble.

She took a breath, pushed. The lock clicked open, the door swung out. Charlie Glass loomed in the rain, in a gray trench coat like hers, baseball cap pulled low. She stepped aside to let him in, saw the Toyota SUV in the alley, wipers on, cargo door open, Smitty at the wheel.

Glass knelt in front of the safe without speaking, took a canvas bag from his coat and shook it open.

She went back out to where the men lay. One of the clerks twisted his face from the floor to look at her. The manager hissed something at him.

"*Silencio,*" she said. "*No se mueva.*"

She went to the window, looked out. The rain was coming down harder, bouncing off the sidewalk. No one walking around out there. Cars splashed by with their headlights on.

A short whistle from the back. She said, "*Relájese. Es casi sobre,*" to the men on the floor and went into the back room again.

The bag was open on the desk, half full of banded stacks of cash. Glass was using a screwdriver to pry open the tray of the DVR recorder on a shelf. It was fed by three surveillance cameras, two in the front, the other back here. She looked around, saw the second recorder on another shelf, in an opposite corner near the floor. She'd missed it the first time.

"Backup," she said, and pointed. He nodded, popped the disc from the open tray. While he worked on the second one, she began opening filing cabinets. The third was full of silver DVDs in slim plastic cases, dates written on them in black marker.

"Got 'em," she said. She'd been in the store a week earlier, would be on that day's surveillance disc. She took all of them to be sure, spilling them into the bag atop the money. He dropped the other two discs in, drew the bag's drawstrings tight, hefted it on his shoulder.

They went out into the rain. Glass tossed the bag into the rear of the SUV, got in behind it, and pulled the cargo door shut. She went around to the passenger side, climbed up. Smitty pulled away without a word. When they reached the end of the alley, he switched his headlights on and made a left onto the street.

"Any problems?" he said.

"No." She slipped off the long dark wig, folded it carefully, put it inside the black plastic garbage bag at her feet. She flipped down the visor and looked in the mirror there, ran her fingers through her close-cropped hair where the wig had flattened it.

They were on a busy street, early rush hour traffic slowed by the rain. Smitty stopped at a red light, and they sat there, the only sound the clicking of the wipers. He began to tap stubby gloved fingers on the wheel, looked up at the light. He was a mechanic, had stolen the SUV the day before from a long-term lot at the airport. The theft likely hadn't been discovered yet, but she knew there was always the risk, the window of exposure before they were safe again.

She leaned over the seat. Glass lay under a blanket in back, the bag in there with him. He was black, bald, and six-four, hard to miss. He'd stay out of sight until they were clear of the city.

"You okay?" she said.

"Yeah."

"A little longer."

When the light changed, they went up a block, then turned onto the big yellow bridge that spanned the Monongahela. A cargo barge chugged along far below them, wake churning behind it. Rain swept the surface of the river.

She powered the window down halfway, felt the wet wind on her face, took her first deep breath since she'd walked into the store. She let it out easy, closed her eyes, willed her heartbeat to slow.

"Man, do I need to take a piss," Smitty said.

When she opened her eyes after a while, they were in the hills, trees on both sides of the road. She rolled her neck to work the stiffness out, adjusted the dashboard vents so the heat blew directly on her legs.

"I mean a *serious* piss," Smitty said.

She looked behind them, no cars. A sign ahead said WEL-COME TO MOON TOWNSHIP.

Five minutes later, they pulled into the gas station, stopping alongside the cracked concrete isle where pumps had once been. She got out, the wind pulling at her, went to the closed bay doors. She caught the handle at the bottom of the right-hand door, heaved up until it was at chest level, then ducked through.

Inside was as they'd left it. Her rented Taurus and Glass's Acura were parked side by side in the other bay, noses out. She pushed the door up the rest of the way, stepped aside as Smitty drove in. When he shut the engine off, she caught the handle, using her weight to drag the door closed.

Smitty left the headlights on, got out. He'd found this place for them, the station abandoned for years, the lifts and hydraulic equipment gone, rusted parts and old tires left behind. She opened the back latch, and Glass climbed out with the bag. Smitty went to the far wall, unzipped, and began to urinate loudly against the concrete.

Glass thumped the bag onto the hood.

"Let's have a look," she said.

He set the DVDs aside, and they counted the money together, passing it between them, lining up the stacks on the still-warm hood. Smitty came back, zipping up.

"Ninety-four five," she said when they were done.

"I've got the same," Glass said. "Shit."

"Ninety-four?" Smitty said. "Are you sure? I thought we were talking close to three hundred?"

"That's what I was told," Glass said. "I don't know what happened."

Crissa looked at the money. Thirty-one five take-home. Hardly worth the trip. No wonder they'd given it up so easy.

"I could tell it wasn't three hundred when I started pulling it out of the safe," Glass said, "but I didn't want to say anything until we counted it. They must have moved some money, made a deposit the night before."

"Or they had another safe somewhere else," she said, "and we missed it."

"God damn it," Smitty said.

"A Friday," Glass said. "They should have been flush. I need to get with my guy, find out what happened."

"Don't bother," she said. "We're not going back."

"God damn it," Smitty said again.

"Come on," she said. "Let's get moving."

She disassembled the Glock, dropped the parts into an open fifty-five-gallon drum of waste oil against the wall, watched them sink. It was the only weapon any of them had carried.

Glass was dividing the money into three piles on the hood, using rubber bands on the loose bills. She popped the trunk of the Taurus, took out an overnight bag. Glass had gotten his own suitcase from the Acura and opened it on the floor. He began filling it with cash. Smitty was still looking at his share of the money on the hood.

"Count it all you want," she said. "It's not going to change. Way it goes sometimes. Nothing for it."

She put her share of the money into the bag, zipped it shut, and carried it back to the Taurus. It went into the trunk alongside another suitcase. Folded beside it was her thigh-length leather coat. She took off the trench coat, dropped it in, put on the leather, and shut the lid.

"It didn't turn out the way we planned," she said, "but that was good work. Both of you."

Smitty loaded his money into a canvas gym bag. Glass stowed his suitcase in the Acura's trunk.

"This got fucked up," he said, "and that's on me. But this isn't a bad thing we got going."

She looked at him.

"You going in front, all innocent like that," he said. "It's under control before they even know what happened. You stick around out here, we can do some more work."

She shook her head.

"You're breaking up a good thing," he said.

"Some other time."

She found a rusted brake shoe, got the bag with the wig out. She dropped the shoe in, tied the top of the bag, and sank it in the waste oil.

"I'll take the discs with me," Glass said. "Burn them."

"Good."

Wind blew against the bay doors. Smitty had wedged the gym bag behind an empty tool cabinet and was stacking tires against it. He'd drop the SUV somewhere in the city, keys in the ignition, then come back for the money, was trusting them enough to hide it in front of them. But he and Glass were locals. If one stole from the other, it would get settled sooner or later. Their world was too small.

"I guess that's it," she said. "See you both down the road."

Glass went to the other bay door, unlatched it, began to push it up. She got into the Taurus, started the engine. As the door rose, she waited to see police cars beyond, flashing lights, men with guns.

The lot was empty. Trees swayed in the wind.

He stepped aside as she pulled out. She turned wipers and headlights on, steered out of the lot and onto the road.

Two miles later, she pulled into a truck stop across from the interstate ramp, parking beside a green Dumpster. She popped the trunk and got out, rain slashing down in the gray half-light. She bundled the trench coat, tossed it through the Dumpster's open hatch, got back behind the wheel. Then she pulled out of the lot and cut across the road and onto the ramp, headed east.

A half hour out of Pittsburgh, the rain turned to snow. She was in mountains now, on curving roads that ran through dry tunnels and then back out into weather. The wind was worse, too. Twice she felt the Taurus drift on the wet black-top.

The snow was blowing almost horizontally, enough of it on the road that she couldn't see the center line anymore. On her left was a high rock wall. To her right, a low guardrail and a long drop into the trees below.

The wipers swished, ice crusting on the blades. Her fingers were tight on the wheel. She'd known the storm was coming, had hoped to beat it, be clear of the mountains before it got serious. Now, with snow on the road and a six-hour drive ahead of her, she could feel the tension building in her back and neck.

Out of a lit tunnel and into a downgrade, and the Taurus's rear end began to slew to the left, into the opposite lane. She turned in the direction of the skid, worked the brake and gas until the car straightened again. She let her breath out slow, her palms damp inside the gloves.

The windshield was fogging, so she switched the defroster to HIGH. The glass began to clear. A car hadn't come from the opposite direction for more than five minutes. The storm was keeping everyone home.

She felt wind push the car, the wheels slip again. Ahead of her, the road curved and another tunnel opened. Lights inside, tiled walls, and she relaxed as she felt the tires grip dry pavement. The tunnel seemed to go on forever. On the other side it was dark as night, snow swirling in her headlights.

The speedometer needle hovered at thirty-five when she passed the scenic outlook, the brown and white police cruiser parked there. She slowed to thirty, looked in the rearview, saw the cruiser swing out after her, rollers on.

She watched as it closed the distance, waiting for it to go around her, pass. It hung there in the rearview, red, blue, and yellow light painting the inside of the Taurus. Then a quick touch of the siren. She signaled, braked, and steered onto the shoulder, felt snow crunch under the tires.

The cruiser pulled up behind her at an angle. Two figures inside. She thought about the money in the trunk. Nothing for it. Nowhere to run.

She switched her hazards on, rested both hands on top of the wheel.

They kept her waiting while they ran the plates. She watched them in the rearview, the driver on his mike. Wind rocked the Taurus. Then both doors opened and they got out on either side—yellow raincoats, Smokey the Bear hats with plastic covers. State police. She watched them come up, one on each side, heads down against the wind. The driver had opened his coat. His right hand rested on a holstered sidearm.

When he reached her window, he made a rolling motion with his left hand. The second trooper played a flashlight beam into the backseat.

She powered down her window. The trooper was young, thick-necked, the bulky outline of a bulletproof vest beneath his uniform shirt.

"License, registration, and insurance please."

"It's a rental," she said. "Hang on, I'll get the contract."

She unsnapped her shoulder belt, flicked the dome light on and leaned across the seat, got the glove box open. The flashlight beam shone through the passenger window, settled on her. She got the yellow rental contract out, then reached into a coat pocket for her wallet. The driver took a step back, his hand on the gun.

She flipped through the wallet, took out the laminated Connecticut driver's license that said her name was Roberta Summersfield, the same name as on the contract.

He took the license and contract without speaking, looked at them briefly, walked back to the cruiser. The other trooper circled the Taurus, fanning the flashlight beam against the bodywork.

She settled her hands atop the wheel again to keep them from shaking. In the rearview, she could see the driver back on the mike. The other trooper watched her through the windshield, expressionless. Snow drifted through the open window, settled on the inside of the door, the sleeve of her jacket, melted.

The driver got out again, came up to her window, the license and contract in his left hand, the right on his weapon.

"Where are you headed, ma'am?"

"Home. Waterbury."

"Where are you coming from?"

"Pittsburgh. Business trip."

He nodded, handed the documents back, looked at the other trooper. He clicked the flashlight off, shook his head.

"We had a hit-and-run on this road earlier," the driver said. "We're checking out all vehicles matching that description."

She slid the license back into its plastic sleeve.

"You've got bigger problems, though," he said.

She looked at him. The other trooper hadn't moved.

"What's that?" she said.

"It'll snow most of the night, ten to twelve inches, likely. We'll be closing some of these roads. Long a drive as you have, I'd strongly suggest you get off at the next exit—that's Salisbury—check into a motel. Roads should be clear by morning."

"Thanks, I'll do that," she said. She put the contract back in the glove box, shut it, breathing again now. "I was starting to get a little nervous out here anyway."

"Half mile ahead on your right. It's a steep exit ramp, so be careful. Have a good night now." He touched his cap.

"I will," she said.

She watched them walk back to the cruiser, get in. Lights still flashing, they U-turned, headed back the way they'd come. She watched their lights in the rearview until they were out of sight.

When she could trust herself to drive, she powered the window up, then pulled back onto the highway and into the storm.

TWO

The motel was a Days Inn just off the highway, the lot almost full. Snow blew past the pole lights. She checked in as Roberta Summersfield, used the credit card she had in that name.

The room was on the second floor. She carried her bags up and two minutes later was in the shower, her clothes strewn on the bathroom floor. The water grew hot quickly, and she ducked under the shower head to let the stream play against the knotted muscles of her neck. The heat began to loosen her shoulders, the tightness in her scalp.

When she was done, she toweled off, then dressed in turtle-neck sweater and jeans. She put the bag with the money up on a shelf in the closet.

Twenty minutes later, she was sitting at the hotel bar, a glass of red wine and the remains of a hamburger in front of her. It was the first she'd eaten since that morning.

At a table to her left were three businessmen in their forties—suit jackets, loosened ties, out of shape. They looked over every few minutes, and she knew they were talking about her. She also knew none of them would have the courage to approach her. It would save her the trouble of shutting them down if they did.

There was a wide-screen TV above the bar, a laugh-tracked sitcom she didn't know. The barmaid took her plate, pointed to her empty wineglass. Crissa said, "Please," and the barmaid took a new glass from the overhead rack, poured from the bottle.

At ten, the news came on. The lead story was the storm, but five minutes later they got to the robbery. A young female reporter stood outside the darkened storefront, bathed in the bright light of the TV camera, snow flitting past, yellow police tape behind her.

Why bother sending someone out there now? Crissa thought. It's all over with.

When the reporter said the robbers had escaped with two hundred thousand in cash, Crissa said, "Bullshit."

The barmaid turned to her. "Excuse me, honey?"

Crissa shook her head. The barmaid looked back at the TV. They'd moved on to sports.

Everyone's scamming, Crissa thought. One way or another. Like Wayne used to say: *Nothing's on the level when the world is round.*

She was feeling the wine, the aftermath of the day's adrenaline rush, the tension of the week. *The way it goes sometimes,* she'd told Smitty, and that was true, but it didn't make her feel any better. Thirty-one five wasn't worth the preparation they'd put into it, the risks they'd taken. It would barely pay her rent for the year. She would put aside part of it anyway, for a trip somewhere warm. Tortola, maybe, or Green Turtle Cay in the Abacos. A Christmas present to herself.

It had become a pattern. A few months of normalcy, relaxation. Then the money at hand would start to run low around the same time she began to get bored. She'd wait for word, a call from Kansas City or St. Louis or Phoenix or a dozen other cities. She'd hear what they had to say. Then, more often than not, she'd be working again—and the cycle would start over. It didn't make for much of a future, she knew. But for now it was the only life she could stand to live.

It was late in the afternoon when she reached New Jersey. She'd called the car service en route, so when she returned the Taurus at the rental agency in Newark, the Town Car was waiting. The Sikh driver loaded her bags in the trunk, asked the address, didn't speak again for the rest of the ride.

The sky was gray and overcast, spitting snow, as they crossed the George Washington Bridge, the city spread out before them. They took the West Side Highway to 125th Street, turned south on Broadway. When they reached 108th he made the left, pulled up in the loading zone in front of her building.

Reynaldo, the doorman, came out to greet her. She paid the driver in cash, tipped him twenty dollars, heard the trunk click open.

Reynaldo already had her bags when she stepped out under the awning, flecks of snow blowing around her. He closed the trunk, tapped it twice, and the Town Car pulled away.

"Welcome back," he said. "How was your trip?"

"Could have been better."

As they started up the steps, a cat raced out from the foyer, slowed when it reached her. It was solid black, its left ear chewed off short and ragged. It eyed her for a moment, then brushed past her legs and into the street.

"I don't know who that belongs to," Reynaldo said. "It's been hanging around here all week. Those cats, they're *mala suerte*. Bad luck."

"I don't need any more of that."

He carried the bags across the marble-floored lobby, pressed the elevator button. It was warm in here, the prewar radiators clanking and hissing. She went to the bank of mailboxes, unlocked the one for 12C. Junk mail, credit card solicitations, utility bills.

When the elevator arrived, she said, "I can take it from here," and gave him a five. She rode up to the twelfth floor, walked down the empty hall, and set her bags in front of the door. Kneeling, she checked the small strip of clear tape that bridged the bottom of the door and the vinyl runner. It was untouched. She keyed the door open, listened for a moment before going in. The clock ticking in the kitchen, nothing else.

She dropped the mail on the foyer table, punched in the security code on the wall keypad, then walked through the apartment, checking rooms. There was no sign anyone had been here while she was gone.

You're tired and paranoid, she thought—and it gets worse each time.

She brought the bags in and locked the door, two dead bolts and a police bar. In the living room, she turned up the thermostat, took off her leather jacket, left it on the futon.

She was feeling the miles now, the residual stress from the last few days.

She was hungry, but almost everything in the refrigerator had gone bad. She made a sandwich of sliced turkey and wilted lettuce stuffed into a stale pita, ate it at the living room window, looking down on 108th Street, Broadway beyond.

Snow was blowing against the glass, gathering on the fire escape. The bar across the street had Christmas lights up already, blinking red and blue bulbs strung above the neon beer signs. A handful of people stood outside, smoking. One by one, they flicked their butts into the street and went back in, passing others coming out to take their place.

Past the corner, she could see the triangle of Straus Park, where Broadway and West End Avenue intersected, snow already covering the grass. A homeless man lay across a bench there, a blanket pulled over him. Catching as much sleep as he could before the police rousted him, sent him back uptown.

She ate half the sandwich, tossed the rest, got a bottle of Château d'Arcins Médoc from the rack atop the refrigerator. She opened it, poured a glass, carried it into the bedroom, and booted up the laptop on her desk. She sipped wine, went to the *Pittsburgh Post-Gazette* Web site. There was an item about the robbery, but nothing that hadn't been in the television report. The four-paragraph story ended with a Crime Stoppers number.

She closed the laptop, brought the glass back into the living room. She turned on the radio in the wall unit. It was already tuned to WQXR, the classical station, and a Bach cello suite filled the room. It was a piece she'd come to recognize but couldn't name.

Sitting cross-legged on the hardwood floor, she unzipped the overnight bag, spilled the cash out. She sipped wine and counted it again. Thirty-one thousand five hundred. Not a dollar more. A lot of risk for little reward.

It was snowing harder now, the wind dancing it around out there in the streetlights. She put the money back in the bag, zipped it shut, got the bottle from the kitchen.

She turned off all the lights in the apartment, sat on the futon, legs tucked under her, bottle on the floor. The lights across the street lit the room in blinking blue and red. It was warmer in here now, the radiators hissing and banging, the reassuring sounds of home.

Alone in the dark, she drank wine and watched the snow.

THREE

When Eddie the Saint walked out of the halfway house for the last time, Terry Trudeau was leaning on the fender of a primer-gray El Camino parked out in front, smoking a cigarette.

Light snow was blowing around, the cracked sidewalk already covered with it. Eddie zipped his state-issue windbreaker higher, shifted the bulging trash bag on his shoulder.

"Hey," Terry said. "I thought they were never gonna let you out of there."

Eddie looked at the El Camino, slowly shook his head. Terry's smile faded.

"Five years inside," Eddie said. "And you expect me to ride out of here in that piece of shit?"

"It's the only—"

"Come over here."

Eddie caught him around the neck, pulled him close. Terry struggled, but Eddie held him there, kissed the top of his head, then pushed him away one-handed. He fell back against the El Camino.

"How long you been out here?"

"Half hour maybe." Terry flicked the cigarette away, raised his hands. Eddie tossed the bag at him.

"Careful with that. You got my whole life in there."

The last time Eddie had seen him, he had a mohawk. Now his hair was short and ragged. He was thinner, wore a sleeveless denim jacket over a hooded sweatshirt. His right eyebrow was pierced.

"Let's get out of here," Terry said. "This place makes me nervous."

Eddie went around to the passenger side. Terry got in, stowed the bag behind the seat, leaned over and popped the door lock.

Eddie looked back at the building where he'd spent the last six months; brick walls, bars on the windows. A black kid with dreadlocks stood outside, smoking a cigarette, watching them. Eddie stared at him until he looked away.

Terry started the engine, exhaust coughing up white in the cold air. Eddie got in. When they pulled away from the curb, Terry said, "How's it feel?"

"It feels good. Drive."

He looked out the window at Newark going by; warehouses, industrial lots with razor-wire fences, blocks of crumbling brownstones. Bare trees, piled garbage.

Terry took a pack of Kools from a jacket pocket, held it out.

"I quit," Eddie said. "Inside. You got any heat in this bitch?"

"Sure." Terry worked the dashboard control, and warm

air blew from the vents. He shook a cigarette from the pack, a slight tremor in his hand, fumbled with the lighter.

"I make you nervous?" Eddie said.

"What do you mean?"

"You need a cigarette to calm your nerves?"

"No, I just . . ."

"Then put 'em away."

Terry tried to fit the cigarette back in the pack, bent it.

"What have you been doing with yourself?" Eddie said.

"Getting by. Worked construction for a while, until things slowed down."

"Construction? You used to be a pretty good burglar. What happened?"

"I haven't done that in a long time, Eddie. I'm out of the game."

"Bullshit. What do you do now?"

"Day work. Whatever comes up."

"Sounds like you're letting your skills go to waste." Eddie reached over, flicked his eyebrow ring. "What's this?"

Terry tilted his head away.

"Aren't you worried someone'll come up to you on the street," Eddie said, "rip that thing out?"

"No one's gonna do that."

"'Cause you're a badass?"

"I didn't say that."

"It looks like shit."

Terry grew silent.

"Sorry," Eddie said. He looked out the window. "It's been a long five years. My social skills are a little rusty."

"It's all right. Where we going?"

"Head south on the Turnpike. I'll tell you when to stop."

"You need to check in with a PO? After you get settled?"

"I'm not on paper anymore, kid. That's why I spent six months in that shithole. No PO. No dropping samples. None of that. I'm free and clear."

"You got a place to crash?"

"Didn't you see me just walk out that door? I got nothing."

"Thing is . . . I'm with Angie now."

"Who's Angie?"

"My old lady. We live together."

"Where?"

"Keansburg. There's not much room, though, you know?"

"Don't worry about it. I'll find a motel."

They were in the Turnpike truck lanes, passing refineries, high-tension towers, oil storage tanks.

"If she wasn't there . . ." Terry said.

"I said don't worry about it."

A tractor-trailer hurtled by, the El Camino quaking in its slipstream. They passed a warehouse with a billboard that read WELCOME TO CARTERET.

"What was it like?" Terry said.

"What?"

"Inside. Was it different this time? I mean, different than it was for us?"

"Same as always. Same bullshit. You do your own time, mind your own business. Just like I taught you."

"Niggers give you a hard time?"

"Not more than once."

"I would have come to see you, but . . ."

"Leave it."

Darkness to the east now, the night coming fast.

"Where do you want to go?" Terry said. "There's motels on the Turnpike, but the ones on Route Thirty-five might be cheaper."

"Keep driving. Couple stops I want to make first."

"I told Angie I'd be back by seven. She's not feeling so hot, so I don't like to leave her by herself. She's been throwing up, can hardly stand without getting nauseous."

"What's wrong, she's so sick you can't leave her alone?"

"She's pregnant."

Eddie shook his head, looked out the window. "And both of you tweakers, right? Outstanding."

"I don't tweak anymore, Eddie. I'm trying to leave that shit behind."

"Whatever. Pull into that rest stop ahead. I want to use the phone."

"I've got a cell."

"I want a pay phone. But while I'm doing that, you can call your old lady."

"Why?"

"To tell her you're not going to make it."

They were parked on a long stretch of road lined with junk-yards and auto body shops, all dark. In the distance, burn-off flares from a refinery lit the sky every few minutes, bursts of blue and yellow flame that made the clouds glow.

"I turned fifty-five inside," Eddie said. "Did you know that?"

"Shit, Eddie, no."

"Yeah, in August. I was one of the oldest motherfuckers in that place, except for the lifers. Fifty-five years old, and beating off in a six-by-ten cell. And even that wasn't giving me any pleasure after a while. Nothing was. Some life, huh?"

Flames glowed against the windshield, faded.

"Tell me again about Casco," Eddie said. "What exactly did he say?"

"Just what I wrote you. That he didn't know me, wouldn't deal with me."

"You told him I sent you?"

"Of course."

"Then that should have been it."

"Hell, Eddie. He *didn't* know me. I don't blame him."

Eddie looked at his watch. It was almost eight.

"What are you going to do?" Terry said.

"Get my money."

"Christ, Eddie, you just got out a couple hours ago. What's the rush?"

"Relax, kid. There's not going to be any trouble. We're all reasonable men."

"How do you know he's there?"

"He's there."

Eddie opened his door. "Come on," he said. "Let's take a walk."

The L&C AUTOBODY sign was dark, but there were lights in the office, someone moving around inside. A flatbed tow truck and a Cadillac were parked out front.

They stood behind the tow truck, away from the light of the streetlamp, cold wind blowing around them.

"He know you're coming?" Terry said.

Eddie didn't answer. A mile away, traffic trundled by on an elevated stretch of turnpike.

"I mean, you called to tell him, right?"

"You should lay off that crank, it makes you squirrelly."

Lights began to go off inside.

Eddie looked around, saw an empty Heineken bottle stuck in a pile of dark snow. He pulled it loose, brushed it clean, wished he had gloves.

Casco came out, a big man in an overcoat, scarf, and hat, and turned to lock the door.

"Wait here," Eddie said and crossed the lot silently. He came up behind Casco, pressed the mouth of the bottle into his back.

"Unlock it again," he said.

Casco froze.

"There's nothing in the office," he said, calm. "We don't do cash business here."

"Unlock it, go on in. Key in the security code. Get it right the first time."

"Eddie? Is that you?"

"Do it."

Casco worked the key in the lock again, opened the door. Eddie pushed him through.

"Code," he said.

The keypad on the wall was blinking red. Casco punched in numbers until there was a faint beep. The light on the keypad turned green.

"Go on through," Eddie said.

"Is this necessary?" He didn't turn.

"Inside." Eddie twisted the bottle. "Your office locked?"

"Yes."

"There another alarm?"

"No."

"Unlock it."

Casco used his keys, opened the door. Eddie walked him in, found the wall switch. Fluorescent bulbs hummed and flickered. Cheap paneling, a metal desk, a gray safe in one corner. Photos of racehorses on the walls.

"What is that?" Casco said. "It's not a pistol."

"It's my dick," Eddie said and pushed him forward lightly. Casco turned, saw the bottle.

"Jesus Christ, Eddie." He let his breath out. "You scared the shit out of me."

"Sorry." Eddie smiled, put the bottle on the desk. "I saw you out there locking up, couldn't resist."

"I thought you were some junkie." He took off his hat, set it on the desk. "You should have called. I could have met you somewhere."

"I did."

"That was you before? Called and hung up? What was that about?"

"Just wanted to make sure you were here. I was passing by, thought I'd stop in."

"When did you get out?"

"About two hours ago."

"And I'm the first person you came to see? I'm honored."

He loosened his coat and scarf, sat heavily in the rolling chair behind the desk.

Eddie looked out, saw Terry peering through the front door, motioned him in.

"Who's out there?" Casco said.

"My partner. You've met him."

"If you say so. You know, it's good to see you and all. But really, that wasn't cool."

"Sorry."

Terry came in, stood in the doorway. Casco said, "Do me a favor, ace. Lock that front door. I don't want anyone walking in off the street."

Terry looked at Eddie. He nodded. Terry went back out.

Casco opened a bottom drawer, took out a bottle of Johnny Walker Black and three plastic glasses.

"Just so you know," he said. "I'm supposed to take Louise out to dinner in the city at nine. We've got reservations."

"Plenty of time." Eddie leaned back against the wall, hands behind him, bounced slightly on the paneling. Casco poured, held the bottle over the third glass, looked up at him. Eddie nodded. Casco poured, capped the bottle again.

When Terry came back in, Casco lifted his glass. *"Salut."*

They drank. It was the first real liquor Eddie had tasted in five years. It went down smooth and warm. Terry coughed.

"What's wrong, kid?" Casco said. "You never had the good stuff before?"

Eddie finished the Scotch, felt the glow spread inside him. He set the glass down. Casco filled it again, then his own.

"So," he said. "What can I do for you?"

"I'm here for my money."

Casco nodded, sat back. "Your money."

"That's right."

"Not a problem. I just need to call my broker, then get to the bank. If you need it all up front, I'll move some around first thing Monday morning, get you a cashier's check."

"Nah." Eddie shook his head, picked up the refilled glass. "Tonight."

"You're shitting me, right?"

"Why would I do that?"

"It's eight o' clock on a Friday. How am I supposed to get your money?"

Eddie drank Scotch, leaned back against the wall.

Casco crossed his arms. "Eddie, with all due respect, I invested that money, as I told you I would. I didn't just bury it in the backyard someplace, where I can dig it up, hand it over."

"Invested where? How?"

"Lots of things. I can show you all the paperwork, the statements. I treated it like I would my own money. I'm a businessman, Eddie, not a bank. I told you that when you gave it to me."

"Forty K." He swirled the remaining Scotch.

"That's what it was," Casco said. "But that was five years ago, Eddie. A lot has changed since then."

"What's that mean?"

"I forget, you've been away. Look, we both took a beating."

"Explain that."

"Christ, Eddie. Even in Rahway you must have heard about what went on in the market. Shit, I know people who

lost their whole life savings. Their 401(k)s, pensions, everything. Everybody got hammered."

"How much did you lose?"

"A lot. But that's not the point."

Eddie drank the rest of the Scotch.

"Look," Casco said. "We talked about this when you
brought it to me. Before you went in. You knew I was going to
put that money to work. You were all for it."

"And now I'm out."

"Eddie, how simply do I have to explain this?"

"Don't fucking patronize me."

"Eddie, I'm not . . ." He gave up. "Listen. You're out, you
need your money. I recognize that. But it isn't forty K, not
anymore."

"How much is it?"

"I'd have to look at the portfolio. But the way the market's
been . . . It's maybe half that by now."

"Half."

"Like I said, I have all the paperwork," Casco said. "Every
dime of it, accounted for. Tino had money with me, too. Ask
him. He'll tell you what it's been like."

"This has nothing to do with Tino."

"What I'm saying is, everybody took a hit. It's just the way
things went."

"Why didn't you tell Terry that? When he came here for the
money?"

"Terry? Who the hell's Terry?" He turned in his chair. "Is
that you, kid?"

He looked back at Eddie. "Listen, put yourself in my place.

Some guy I've never seen before comes in off the street, tells me he's with you. I'm supposed to hand him ten grand of your money?"

"I needed it. For a lawyer."

"Then you should have called, told me that. Jesus, Eddie, kid comes in here, sores on his arms, nose running, scratching the whole time. He was so methed out, I wasn't going to give him shit."

Terry put his half-filled glass on the desk. "I'll wait outside."

"Hey, kid, no offense," Casco said.

"No," Eddie said. "Stay."

Terry turned, hovered in the doorway.

"He used my name," Eddie said. "That should have been enough."

"I think you're being unreasonable," Casco said.

"Am I?"

"This isn't some street-corner bullshit. This is business."

Eddie scratched his chin. He'd shaved this morning, but the stubble was back.

"You're right," he said after a moment. "It's business. I apologize. What's in the safe?"

"What?"

"The safe right there. What's in it? How much?"

"Petty cash. Four hundred maybe. Yours if you want it, but it's hardly worth opening the thing up. Give me a day or two, and I'll shake loose as much of your money as I can. Get it all back in cash, if that's what you want."

Eddie looked at Terry. "What do you think?"

Terry shrugged.

"Listen, kid, I'm sorry," Casco said. "Like I was saying, I didn't know you from Adam. I meant no disrespect, and I'm sorry if I gave you a hard time." He looked at Eddie. "Better?"

"The safe."

"Eddie, stop acting like this. Let's get Tino on the phone right now. The three of us can talk it over."

"Open it."

"Why are you doing this? I've always shown you respect. Why can't you do the same?"

Eddie put his empty glass on the desk.

"Christ," Casco said. "If it'll make you feel better."

He rolled the chair to the safe, took a pair of reading glasses from his shirt pocket, put them on. He bent over the dial, started to work it.

Eddie came around the desk behind him. Casco got the combination wrong the first time, had to wipe his palm on his pants leg, start over.

"You're making me nervous standing back there," he said.

Eddie put his hands on Casco's shoulders, kneaded the muscles there.

"Easy," he said. "Relax."

Casco hunched to break the grip. "I'm fine."

Eddie took his hands away, stepped back. Casco worked the dial a final time, started to pull up on the handle.

"Hold on," Eddie said. "Anything else in there I should know about before you open it?"

"No. Enough with the drama, all right?" He pulled on the door.

"Back away," Eddie said.

Casco rolled his chair to the side. Eddie knelt. Ledger books inside, a thick manila accordion folder. He rifled through papers.

Casco looked at Terry. "What, you don't talk?"

Eddie undid the elastic tie on the folder, opened it, saw banded money inside. He dumped it out on the floor. Stacks of bills, fifties and twenties.

"It's not as much as it looks, Eddie. A few grand maybe . . ."

Where the folder had been was a dark automatic and a box of shells. He drew the gun out. It was a Star 9, small but solid, with ridged grips. He ejected the magazine, saw it was loaded.

"I didn't even know that was in there," Casco said. "I swear. It belongs to one of my guys. He carries it when he works late."

Eddie set the gun and box atop the safe, then stood, knees popping. He was feeling the cold in his joints. He pressed his palms against his lower back, stretched.

"Come on, Eddie. Enough of this. You're out of line and you know it."

Eddie toed the banded bills.

"How much is that?"

"Shit, I don't know. I put it in there as I need to. I don't count it every time. It can't be much."

"Looks like ten, maybe fifteen K."

"If you say so."

"Which makes you a liar."

"If you want it, take it. A down payment on what I owe you."

Eddie picked up the gun, stood away from the safe. "Count that," he said to Terry. "I can't bend over anymore."

Terry gathered the money. They watched as he counted,

lips moving, thumbing through the bills, lining the stacks up on the desk. He went through them a second time and said, "Twenty-five thousand."

Eddie looked at Casco. "Petty cash?"

"Like I said, I don't keep track of what's in there."

Eddie picked up the gun. "This is nice."

"Eddie, this is bullshit. How long have we known each other? Twenty years? Don't you think we're a little old for this shit?" His face was sallow in the fluorescent light.

Eddie shoved the folder toward Terry with his foot. "Put it back in there."

"I really think we should call Tino," Casco said.

"Tell me again. What you're going to do Monday."

Casco exhaled, the tension draining from him. "First thing in the morning, I go to my broker, get a printout on everything, so you can see where it all went, to the penny. I'll move the money around, get you a cashier's check on my personal account."

"I want cash."

"Yeah, I guessed. I'll cash the check myself. The transfers won't go through for a couple days, but I'll give you the money out of my own account. You won't have to wait."

"Good. Anything else in that safe I missed?"

"Nothing. Just papers, bookkeeping."

"Let me have a look at one of those ledger books."

"They wouldn't mean anything to you."

"I'm curious anyway."

Casco sighed, rolled his chair back to the safe.

"Tino's not going to like this," he said.

"That a threat?"

"No. I just don't know why we're doing this."

"Humor me."

Casco leaned forward, brought out a red ledger book bound lengthwise with a rubber band. He looked at Eddie, put it atop the safe.

"What's that in the back?" Eddie said.

"Where?"

"In the back, on that shelf."

"I don't see anything."

"Get down there and take a look."

"Eddie, I got a bum knee."

"You're younger than me. You'll be fine."

"I swear, Eddie . . ." He knelt, winced. "I don't see anything."

"All the way in the back there."

When Casco leaned forward, his face in the safe, Eddie put a foot between his shoulder blades to hold him there, shot him twice in the back of the head.

Terry jumped. The sound of the shots echoed off the paneling. Brass clinked on the floor.

Eddie took his foot away. Casco's body slumped forward, then rolled slowly to the side, face up. Terry looked away.

Eddie tucked the still-warm gun into his belt, put the box of shells in his jacket pocket. Then he leaned over, tugged out Casco's wallet, tossed it on the desk.

"See what's in there, too."

When he got no response, he looked over, saw Terry frozen, white-faced.

"What?" Eddie said.

Terry shook his head, said nothing.

Eddie pointed at the folder. "Take that. Half of it is yours."

When Terry didn't move, Eddie went over to him, cupped the back of his neck, squeezed.

"Look at me," he said. "I need you to get your shit together."

Terry nodded, still looking at Casco's body. Eddie let go.

"Get one thing straight," he said. "This wasn't about money. It was about principle."

FOUR

"It's beginning to look a lot like Christmas," Walt Rathka said.

Crissa set the FAO Schwarz bag beside his desk, unwound her scarf. Sleet rattled the big office window, the clamor of horns drifting up from Fifth Avenue, twelve stories below.

"Have a seat," he said. "Get dry. Hang those things up. Sorry Monique's not here to take them."

He went back to his chair. He was in his late fifties, wore a suit and tie, red suspenders. She could smell his cologne, knew it went for about eighty dollars an ounce.

"When did you get back?" he said.

"Yesterday."

She settled into the red leather chair in front of his desk. She had a wine headache from the night before, had finished most of the bottle. It had relaxed her, but not enough to sleep, so she'd taken half a Lunesta. She was feeling the aftereffects now, a tightness around her eyes, a drowsiness two cups of herbal tea at the West Way hadn't cured.

"Successful shopping trip?" he said.

"Not very. I was able to get something for the twins, though."

"Generous of you. My daughter thinks I'm spoiling them."

"That's what kids are for."

"What my wife says. Any complications?"

"None I know of."

"Good. I worry about you sometimes, Crissa."

"Don't. Go ahead, have a look."

He drew the bag closer, took out the stuffed animals, a blue dog and pink rabbit. Beneath was a layer of tissue paper. He pulled it back to expose the banded stacks of money, tilted the bag for a better look.

"It's not much," she said. "I'd hoped to do better."

He replaced the paper and the stuffed animals. "I'm sure the twins will enjoy them."

"How's our project going?"

"The Alabama one? As planned. Construction should begin early next year. Or the next. Hard to tell. Companies are doing well, though, stable as can be. In fact . . ."

He opened a drawer, slid a legal-sized envelope across the blotter. Inside was a pale blue check for twenty thousand dollars, from a land development company in Anniston. It was made out to Christine Steiner. She kept a Bank of America account in that name.

"Your quarterly consulting fee," he said. "Legal and accounted for. You can do whatever you like with it."

"Thanks." She closed the envelope, nodded at the bag. "You should put that someplace."

"I will. You look tired, Crissa."

"Long drive. Bad weather."

"You staying in the city for a while?"

"For the immediate future. Unless something comes up."

"Good. I heard from the Realtor in Connecticut. She says the Hammersteins are about ready to make a decision on the house. I'm told your offer is near the top of the list. You're still interested, right?"

"If the terms are right. If they keep screwing around, I'll walk away. There are other houses."

"That's what I told her. She said they wanted to know more about your background. I said, if you're willing to put sixty percent down, especially in this economy, what do they care about your background? They'll come around, I think."

"What about the Texas situation?"

He sat back.

"Well, that . . ." he said.

"I'm going down there to see him soon. I want something to tell him."

He crossed his arms. "I'm afraid it doesn't look good at the moment."

"Define that."

Sleet slashed the window.

"He's had some issues since he's been in custody there, as you know," he said. "There was a fight with another inmate."

"That was self-defense."

"I'm sure it was. Even so, it'll hurt him at the parole hearing in March. My colleague down there says he has an in at the statehouse that could help us, but he wants more money up front to get his man properly motivated, grease the necessary wheels."

"You mean palms."

"That, too."

"This lawyer, you trust him?"

"As far as it goes. Whether his man has as much clout with the Texas Department of Criminal Justice as he'd like us to believe, I don't know. I guess we won't find out until the hearing."

"How much this time?" she said.

"For his man at the statehouse? Two fifty, he says. I'm guessing that means two for his man and fifty for him."

"With all we've given him already . . ."

"I know. It adds up. And if I were licensed to practice in Texas, I'd be down there right now myself, shaking trees and working the angles. So to a certain extent we have no choice. We have to trust him."

"Two hundred and fifty grand's a lot. I don't know if I could put that much together right away. Not in cash."

"It's your call, as always."

She looked out the window at the rain.

"Wayne turns fifty-one in April," she said.

"I know."

"That place is killing him."

"I can try to get him down to two hundred, but I don't know if he'll go for it."

Goddamn Texas, she thought. It would never let her loose.

"He's got seven years left on his bid," she said. "If he doesn't make parole, he's going to die in there. I'm not going to let that happen. Whatever we have to do, whatever it costs, that's what we'll do."

"Understood."

"Tell your man he'll get the two fifty. But push him for some reassurances, some names."

"He might be reluctant to do that."

"Push him anyway."

"Consider it done."

She stood. He got up, went to the door, waited as she put on her jacket and scarf. The envelope went into an inside pocket.

"I'll call you as soon as I hear back," he said. "You have a new number yet?"

"Soon. I'll call, give it to Monique."

He opened the door for her, put out his hand. She shook it.

"When you talk to him . . ." he said.

"Yes?"

"Tell him we're doing our best."

"I will," she said.

She took the subway uptown, the 1 train packed with tourists and holiday shoppers. No empty seats. She worked her way to the end of the car, grasped the vertical pole. Across from her sat two Asian girls, barely in their teens, clutching hard plastic cello cases. To her left stood a well-dressed man in his forties, suit and overcoat, dark hair flecked with gray. He reached up to grip the pole above her head, gave her a bemused smile and looked away.

Four people got off at 50th Street, but twice as many

squeezed on, forcing her closer to the man in the suit. Soon she was sweating freely from the heat in the car, the headache still nagging her.

At 59th, more people crowded in, including a man in his twenties wheeling an upright bicycle. The doors closed twice on the rear tire, bonged, and opened again. He pulled the bike in farther, embracing the frame like a lover, people wordlessly shifting to make room. As the doors closed, he met Crissa's eyes, then looked away. She studied him anyway, half from practice, half from boredom. He was shaven-headed, wore glasses with thin black frames. The Moby look, a style half the men in the city under fifty seemed to affect these days.

The train lurched out of the station, people swaying with the motion, and the man in the suit bumped hard against her. "Excuse me," he said. He reset his grip on the pole, his hand brushing hers for an instant.

At 66th, the Asian girls got off, maneuvering their cello cases through the crowd and onto the platform. Their seats were taken instantly. When the doors opened at 72nd, there was a communal groan as more people pressed in. She caught a glimpse of a cop on the platform, a leashed German shepherd lying at his feet.

They pulled out of the station, and as the car accelerated, the man in the suit bumped her again. He looked at her and smiled. "Sorry."

Enough of this, she thought. Too many stops to go to put up with it. She let go of the pole, moved through the car, squeezed past the man with the bicycle, reached the connecting door and pulled it open.

The next car was no better. She found a spot at the far end, beside a Mexican worker listening to an iPod. He shifted to give her room. She gripped the pole with her left hand, watched the tunnel walls blur past the windows.

Seventy-ninth. Four more stops to go, three if she got off at 103rd and walked. People filed out of the car, and an equal number seemed to get back on, filling the gaps they'd left. An old woman sneezed loudly.

Crissa faced the doors, her headache worse now. Someone bumped into her from behind, drew away. She turned to the left, saw the man in the suit. He met her eyes, smiled.

She looked away. The car was too crowded for her to move any farther. The train swung into a jostling turn, lights flickering, people holding on, and the man closed the distance, bumped her hip again, held it longer this time before pulling away.

"Back off," she said. When she turned to him, there were only inches between them. He pointed down. She looked, saw the erection pushing through the material of his pants.

She felt heat in her face, looked away. No one else around them had noticed their exchange. She tried to move to her right, couldn't.

The car rattled and swayed as it entered another curve, picking up speed. She knew what was coming, how the vertex of the turn would bunch everyone together before the track straightened. She flexed her fingers, gripped the pole tighter.

The lights blinked again. In her peripheral vision, she saw the man draw back, ready to let the momentum of the car take him. He knew what was coming, too.

The train swung wide, and as he swayed toward her she let go of the pole, brought her left elbow around and down hard, twisting her hips into it. She felt the impact, his nose giving way. He fell back as the train came out of the turn, the crowd holding him up. People pushed him away in irritation.

The train slid into the station, the doors hissing open. She stepped out onto the platform, looked back, people streaming around her. She saw the man fall in stages, his eyes unfocused, blood pouring from his nose. He slumped to the floor. A Hispanic girl in a pink vinyl jacket got on, looked down at him, said, "Gross." The doors closed, and the train pulled away.

Crissa went up the stairs and out onto Broadway. Almost dark now, the rain slanting down.

Halfway down the block, she noticed the blood smear on her left elbow. She got a Kleenex from her pocket, wiped at the leather until it was clean.

Crossing Broadway, she turned north into the wind, dropped the bloody tissue into a trash basket. Eighty-sixth Street. Twenty-two blocks to go. She tightened her scarf. The walk will do you good, she thought. You can use the exercise.

FIVE

The next day the clouds had lifted, the morning clear and cold. She had breakfast at the West Way, read most of the *New York Times* over eggs and bacon, got a second cup of tea to go.

Back in the apartment, restless and caffeinated, she put on her red and black Puma track suit, stretched on the living room floor. She needed to run, to clear her head, to think.

When she left the lobby, the black cat with the torn ear was lurking behind a stone planter. It fled when it saw her.

It felt good to hit the street. The sky was bright blue, the air sharp. She jogged south along Broadway for a block, the street smells strong; scorched pretzels, falafel, bus exhaust. All that remained of the snow was gray sludge in the gutters.

Crossing at the light, she headed west on 107th to Riverside Drive, picking up speed on the downhill slope. At the corner, she jogged in place, waiting for the light to change, then headed into the park.

Sunlight glared off the Hudson as she ran south along the promenade, weaving around runners and bicyclists, putting on speed. A cluster of pigeons flew away as she neared them.

She measured off the half mile from memory, then turned, jogged in place for a moment, and started back, her breath clouding.

She wondered how long it would take to raise two hundred and fifty thousand, and what it would buy her from the lawyer in Texas. Or if it was all just a scam, money for empty promises and no results. Money she would never get back.

She went up to 114th, dodging rollerbladers, then left the park, crossed Riverside again to take the long way home. Running east on 114th, she passed chattering groups of Columbia students, people walking dogs, then turned south on Amsterdam.

The neighborhood was different here, less gentrified. A group of Dominican teens outside a liquor store yelled something at her. She ignored them, fought the urge to speed up, not wanting them to see her react.

At 112th and Amsterdam, she slowed as she always did, looked across at Diego's. It was the last bodega in the neighborhood, the plate glass window crowded with signs for calling cards, money wiring services, cigarettes. There in the lower left-hand corner, the Corona beer poster, a sweating amber bottle beneath a palm tree. Just another sign in the cluttered window—but today this one was upside down.

She kept going, did the last four blocks and turned back onto 108th, slowing now as she neared her building.

The sign was like that only two or three times a year, a message from Hector. It meant only one thing. Work.

Her phone was almost out of minutes, so she got another from the desk in the bedroom and broke it out of its plastic package. She bought them whenever she could, always in different places, and with cash.

She activated the phone, punched in Hector's number, got his voice mail. She said, "Me," and ended the call.

When he called back, she was on a yoga mat in the living room, stretching the soreness out of her legs.

"You in town?" he said.

"Just got back. Saw your message."

"Up for lunch?"

"Heavy lunch or light lunch?"

"Light now, maybe heavier later if you like what they're serving."

"When?"

"Free now?"

She looked at her watch. One thirty.

"An hour," she said. "Same place as last."

"See you there," he said and ended the call.

The Hop Ling restaurant was in a warren of short, crooked streets off Mott, in between a toy shop and a store that sold nothing but ornamented purses.

She went down the street level stairs, shouldered open the door. A wave of heat and scent hit her—fried food, steamed rice. Inside the low-ceilinged room were booths, a plywood counter, a roped-off table area in the back.

Hector was in a booth in the far corner, facing the door, wearing a green flight jacket. He was the only non-Asian in the room. Half the other booths were occupied, people eating purposefully.

She had to sidestep fast-moving waiters on her way over. The kitchen doors flew open and shut, smatterings of urgent Cantonese coming from inside.

She slipped into the booth across from him. There was a silver teapot on the table, two ceramic cups, a pair of oversized menus.

"I didn't order," he said. "I was waiting for you."

She shifted to get a sight angle on the door. He opened his menu flat on the table. As always, her eyes were drawn to the Gothic script tattoo on his neck, his brother Pablo's initials, birth and death dates. Pablo had started out working with Wayne, then gone on to run his own commercial burglary crew, with Hector as his contact man. He'd been killed by federal marshals trying to serve a fugitive warrant on him in an Atlantic City motel.

"How was the road trip?" Hector said.

"Not so good."

"Were the sights exaggerated?"

"A little. Nobody's fault."

"That's too bad. Charlie's information is usually accurate."

"Way it goes," she said. "Nothing for it."

She took an envelope from her inside jacket pocket, slid it under his menu, held up three fingers to show him how much. Whenever he steered her to work, she gave him ten percent of her take-home. It was the arrangement they'd had for the last three years, since she'd come north.

"That bad, huh?" he said.

"That bad."

He slipped the envelope into his jacket.

An elderly waiter came over, pulled a pencil from behind his ear, and stood pad in hand. She wasn't hungry, but it would attract attention to be here without food. She ordered hot and sour soup. Hector pointed to a special on the handwritten card in the menu's plastic liner. The waiter took their menus, left without speaking.

"I figure I better eat," Hector said. "I have to go out to Paterson later on, help my brother-in-law move some furniture. Like my back's not fucked up enough."

"How are the girls?"

"Getting big. Elita turns seven next month. She's got her First Holy Communion coming up this spring, at Saint Anthony's. Already her mother's worried about it. I said, '*Ay por dios*, let's get through Christmas first.'" He patted his jacket. "This will help."

"I was surprised to get your message. I've only been back a couple of days."

"I know. But I didn't want to wait either."

He poured tea, looked at her. She nodded, and he filled her cup, steam rising up.

"I don't know that I'm up to traveling again yet," she said.

"That's what I figured. But if I didn't think it was worth your time . . ."

She sat back to listen.

"You remember that guy from Staten Island? Runs an electronics store?"

She shook her head.

"Bald guy. Big dude. Little beard here." He stroked his chin.

Stimmer. "Yeah, okay."

"He's looking for associates for an out-of-area opportunity."

"He say what it was?"

"No, just that it would be worth it. He bad news to you?"

"No more than anyone."

Their food arrived, the waiter dropping the steaming plates in front of them without a word and vanishing as quickly. Hector ripped the paper off his chopsticks, pulled them apart.

"He's planning a seminar soon. Asked if I knew anyone with experience who wanted to attend."

"He mention my name?"

He shook his head, pushed rice and chicken around his plate, the smell of it wafting up.

"No names. But he knows who I talk to."

She took noodles from a bowl, crushed them into her soup.

"What makes you think it's worth my time?"

"He said it might be a Stage Seven project."

"I've heard that before."

Stage Seven meant seven figures or more. She blew on her soup, sipped a spoonful. It made her eyes water.

"Where at?"

"He didn't say."

"Where's the seminar?"

"Across the river, he says. Not far. I didn't get all the details."

Jersey. She frowned. She didn't like doing anything close to home, even prep work.

"Is that where the project is?"

"I don't think so. If I thought it was, I wouldn't have bothered you with it."

She stirred her soup. Even if the figures were exaggerated, Stimmer was solid. Depending on how big the crew was, it might be worth it. She thought about the lawyer in Texas.

"I might look into it," she said. She spooned soup.

"I'll get back in touch with him," he said. "If it still sounds good, I'll call you."

"He say how many associates he was looking for?"

"No. Just that the work-to-reward ratio was high. Not very labor-intensive. I got the impression he meant three, maybe four."

She drank tea. Stimmer was a pro, but underestimating the work involved and crew needed was a common mistake. Greed sometimes led to undermanning. The times that happened, she'd tried to convince the organizers otherwise. If she couldn't, she walked.

She'd yet to put together a crew herself, though. She dealt almost exclusively with men, and many of them refused to take direction from a woman. When Wayne had run crews, she was his right hand, gave orders, made suggestions, and the others went along with it. Now she was on her own.

"So I'll tell him maybe?" Hector said.

"If I like what I hear. I want your sense of it first. If you get details and don't think it's worth it, that'll be it. I don't want the complication of hearing his pitch and then saying no. Makes people nervous."

"He might not want to tell me. Might only want to talk to you."

"Then he's out of luck," she said.

SIX

When Terry pulled up in front of the house, there was a banged-up Schwinn on the open porch.

"Whose bike?" Eddie said

"It belongs to Cody," Terry said. "He's a friend."

"He always hang around your old lady when you're not home?"

"He stays here sometimes."

"Whatever."

They got out. It was late afternoon, the sky gray. Eddie had used some of Casco's money to buy new clothes, left the old ones in a Dumpster behind the motel. He wore a black trench coat and white roll-neck sweater, left the coat open. He liked the way it hung on him, like a duster.

They went up the slate path. The porch creaked under them.

"How long you lived here?" Eddie said.

"Couple months. Angie knows the owner."

"Knows or blows?"

"What do you mean?"

"Never mind."

When Terry opened the door, Eddie frowned at the smell that came out. Marijuana, fried food, and body odor.

They stepped into a hallway, stairs to the left, living room to the right. There was a sleeping bag on the floor there, a couch with threadbare arms, a recliner leaking stuffing. Empty beer bottles on a coffee table.

"Christ," Eddie said. "Leave the door open."

"Terry?" A woman's voice from upstairs, then slow footsteps coming down. Eddie looked up. The woman had stringy blond hair, wore faded jeans and a T-shirt. She'd been pretty once.

"Angie," Terry said. "This is Eddie. I told you about him."

Eddie nodded at her. She put a hand on her belly, as if to protect it.

"Hey," a man's voice called from down the hall. "Close the fucking door."

Eddie turned to Terry. He was looking at the floor.

Eddie went down the hall to the kitchen. A man with long, greasy hair and a Metallica T-shirt was sitting at a table, spooning soup from a bowl. He looked up when Eddie came in. He had big arms, blue snake tattoos curling around veiny biceps. He ate prison style, elbows on both sides of the bowl, protecting his food.

"Who the fuck are you?" he said.

"You Cody?"

"Who's asking?"

Eddie looked around. The stove was stained with food, the sink full of dishes. "Out."

Cody looked at him, lifted another spoonful of soup, taking his time. Terry was watching from the hallway.

"You got ten seconds," Eddie said. "Starting now."

"You need to chill, pops. Who do you think you're talking to?"

"Nine."

"Terry, who is this dude?"

"Eight."

Eddie came around the table, took the bowl, and dumped it into the sink, soup splashing the dishes already there. Cody pushed away from the table, stood. He was a full head taller than Eddie, his chest and shoulders thick from a prison weight room.

"What the fuck is your problem, man? You want to get your ass tore up?"

"Seven."

"You better—"

"One." Eddie drove a heel into the outside of Cody's knee, his weight behind it. It snapped the leg in, and Cody cried out, bent. Eddie brought a knee up hard into his face, then head-locked him before he could fall. He dragged him through the kitchen and into the hall. Terry stepped aside. Angie watched from the stairs.

Cody was starting to flail by the time they reached the door. Eddie tightened his grip, cutting off his air. He slung him out onto the porch, then gave him a two-handed shove that sent him over the steps and onto the slate path. He landed hard on his side.

"Five seconds to be on your way," Eddie said.

Cody rolled to his hands and knees. Blood dripped from

his nose to the slate. Eddie picked up the bike, lifted it chest high, and flung it. It hit him, knocked him back on his side.

"Four."

Cody looked at him, got slowly to his feet. "Man, I think you broke my nose." His voice was thick. "You didn't have to do that."

"Hold on," Eddie said. He went back in the house, got the sleeping bag. It stank of sweat and smoke. He brought it out, tossed it off the porch.

"Take that with you. If I ever see you here again, I'll break your back."

Cody wiped his face, picked up the sleeping bag, began to roll it.

"Three," Eddie said. He came down the porch steps.

Cody tucked the half-rolled sleeping bag under his arm. He righted the bike, walked it to the sidewalk quickly. He dropped the sleeping bag, had to lean to pick it up, the bike almost falling over.

"Two," Eddie said.

Cody got on the bike, started to pedal fast, unsteady at first. He looked back once. Eddie watched him ride away.

He went back in. Angie hadn't moved.

"We're going out," he said to her. "While we're gone, clean this shithole up. Start with that kitchen."

She looked at Terry. He looked away.

"What are you waiting for?" Eddie said to her. "Get at it."

They were at the bottom of a dead-end street, sitting on a guardrail, looking out at the bay. Wind blew cold off the water. In the distance, the lights of fishing boats on the darkening horizon.

"This baby," Eddie said. "You sure it's yours?"

Terry looked at him. "Why would you say something like that?"

"Just asking. Something to think about, though, you know. Before you start rearranging your life."

"It's mine."

"Sorry I mentioned it."

"Angie's a good kid."

"I'm sure she is. That guy was punking you, though. Whether you knew it or not."

Terry looked off at the water.

"I don't know what you've been doing since I've been away," Eddie said, "but I don't like what I've seen so far. You want to ride with me again, we need to get some things straight."

Terry nodded, looked down.

"You can't go around with me looking like you do," Eddie said. "Take that money I gave you, buy some clothes. For the girl, too."

"Okay."

"You want people's respect, you have to respect yourself first."

Terry got lighter and cigarettes out. With the wind, it took him four tries to get one lit.

"I called Tino today," Eddie said.

"What did he say?"

"He might have something for us soon. I'm going to meet him later this week. He owes me. He knows that."

"Why?"

"Because the last favor I did him cost me five years. That dealer I shot in the knee in Passaic, he was pushing up on one of Tino's niggers. Tino paid for the lawyer, yeah, but I'm the one did the time. And for the appeal, I had to hire another one myself. You think he'd leave his idiot son, or one of his *cumbadis,* twisting in the wind like that?"

"I thought you guys were tight."

"Tino's not tight with anyone. He's a fucking paranoid individual. Always has been, and I've known him thirty years. And I'm only half Italian, you know? So he trusts me even less. Half Italian, half spic, and I don't speak either."

Terry blew smoke out.

"You don't look too happy," Eddie said. "Way you've been living, I thought you'd be glad to see me."

"I am, it's just . . ."

"What?"

"I don't know. I didn't expect all this shit to start over again so soon, I guess."

"What shit? Didn't I put twelve grand in your pocket the other day? I thought you'd be happy making white man's money again."

"I just didn't understand it, that's all."

"Understand what?"

"If he was promising to get all your money back in a couple days, if he could actually do it, why kill him?"

"You been stewing about that? That what's been bothering you?"

"I was just thinking. If he was offering to pay you . . ."

"He wasn't going to pay me. Not after I braced him like that. He was going to shine me on, then find some way to weasel out of it. Go crying to Tino. Or, if he grew balls, pay someone to whack me."

"Why?"

"Because he was scared of me. Sometimes, when you get hard with people, you have to finish it right there, whether they deserve it or not. Because there's always the chance they'll come back at you somewhere down the road. That twenty-five K was all I was ever going to get out of him, and we both knew it."

Terry tossed his cigarette into the water.

"You saw it when we were on the tier together," Eddie said. "Guys don't get stabbed because they owe money and can't pay. Guys get stabbed because they *lent* money, and the poor fucker who borrowed it is afraid what'll happen if he doesn't pay, so he makes the first move. Casco would have bided his time, given me a few bucks here and there. Then he would have moved on me. No way around it."

"He used Tino's name."

"I stopped living my life worrying about what Tino thinks. He'll get over it."

"What are you going to do now?"

Eddie stood. "Make some moves. See what I can get going again. Feels like I've been away a long time."

"It was worse this time, wasn't it?"

"In Rahway? Only thing I missed was having your sweet ass around to do my laundry, make my bed."

"Cut it out."

Eddie put an arm around his neck, squeezed, tugged him off the rail. Terry pushed at him, and Eddie laughed, released him, shoved him gently away.

"Seriously, kid. Think about it. Three years in the same cell together, I could have fucked you any time I wanted. But I never did. I was a gentleman."

"Don't even joke about that, man."

"Better me than some brothers, right? One of them holding a shank to your throat while the others pull a train."

"That shit ain't funny."

"I'm just screwing with you. Come on, let's go."

They started back toward the house.

"You want to come in?" Terry said. "I think there's some beers in the refrigerator."

"I go back in there, I'll never get the stink off me. Some other time. Drive me back to the motel."

When they reached the El Camino, Eddie said, "Your woman. How pregnant is she?"

"Four months, about. She's just starting to show."

"She got a doctor?"

"The clinic. There's one in Keyport."

"Fuck that. Take that money, find a real doctor. His eyes'll light up when he sees that cash. If anybody asks, tell them you won it at the track. They won't turn you away. I guarantee that."

"Thanks."

Eddie put a hand on his shoulder, squeezed.

"Stick with me, kid," he said. "Things are about to get a lot better for both of us. I can feel it."

SEVEN

Crissa parked the rented Honda in the trees, looked up the long gravel driveway to the farmhouse. Lights on inside, two cars parked in the side yard, a dark barn beyond.

She slipped out of the car, made her way up through the trees. She wore a black Aran sweater, jeans, and boots. In the right-hand pocket of her leather jacket was a snub-nosed .38. Wayne had given it to her not long after they'd met. She'd gotten it from the safe deposit box at the bank on 101st that afternoon. She never kept guns in the apartment.

A light over the side door lit the two cars. One was a blue Ford Focus, Jersey plates, a rental. The second was a sleek black BMW with tinted windows and New York plates.

She checked the barn first. A side wall and part of the roof had collapsed. Nothing inside but rubble. She moved back toward the house, laid her hand on the Ford's hood, could feel the warmth through her glove. The BMW was as cold as the night.

Curtains on the side window. She could see a figure moving inside, hear voices. She took out the .38. It was nickel plated with mother-of-pearl grips, the serial number removed with acid. It was untraceable, had never been used in a crime.

She tucked it in the Y of a dead tree. If it was a setup inside, law, she didn't want it on her. This way, if she had to run, needed it then, she'd be able to reach it quick.

She knocked at the side door. Silence, then the scrape of chairs. She stepped back. Footsteps inside and then Stimmer was there, peering through the glass, right hand hidden behind his leg. He wore a commando sweater under a dark parka. He looked past her, to right and left. She waited while he worked locks.

"Crissa," he said when the door was open. "Long time."

He stepped aside as she came in. He was bulky through the neck and shoulders, a weight lifter. The last work they'd done together, a supermarket payroll in Muncie, Indiana, had been three years ago. He'd run it well, and she'd come home with seventy-eight grand, one of her first times working without Wayne.

He locked the door again, led her down a hall into an ancient kitchen. There was an oversized refrigerator with an old-fashioned latch, the enamel yellow with age. Patches of the linoleum floor were worn through to the wood.

Chance sat at the kitchen table. He smiled when he saw her, rocked back on his chair. "Hey, Red."

"Hey, Bobby. Good to see you."

"Same here. I feel better now."

"You two know each other already," Stimmer said. "I should have guessed."

He set a dark automatic atop the refrigerator. The gun bothered her. There was no need for it.

"Who else?" she said.

"That's it," Stimmer said. "Just three."

It was as cold inside as out. Chance wore a blue down vest over a red flannel shirt buttoned at the wrists. He had full-sleeve tattoos beneath, she knew, elaborate designs he'd paid thousands for in Thailand. The last time she'd seen him, he'd had a ponytail. Now his dark hair was shorter, parted in the middle.

"Good thing you dressed warm," he said.

She looked at Stimmer.

"Someone live here?"

"Not anymore." He dragged a chair over to the table for her. "It's coming down soon. They're going to build condos or some shit here if the economy ever turns around. They left the power on, but no heat."

He straddled a chair at the head of the table. Crissa sat to his right, Chance across from her.

"You're looking good," Chance said.

"Thanks. I see you're keeping on."

"Beats working, like Wayne used to say. What do you hear from him?"

"You know the way it is. One day at a time. Going down to see him soon."

She and Chance had worked together twice, a diamond broker outside Jacksonville and an armored car in Cincinnati, both with teams Wayne led. Clean work, solid, with no blowback.

She ran a hand under the surface of the table, felt knots and bulges in the wood, no wires.

"Warmer where we're going," Stimmer said.

"*If* we go," Chance said.

"Tell it," she said.

"It's a sweetheart," Stimmer said. "Fort Lauderdale card game. High rollers. A million, maybe more, on the table."

"That's hard to believe," she said.

Chance smiled. "My first reaction, too."

"But?"

"Game's new," Stimmer said. "Unprotected. It started with some players from the Seminole casino over in Hollywood. They wanted a looser environment, higher stakes. Poker drawing amateurs the way it is these days, they set up the game to fleece the wannabe big-timers. That's why it's in a hotel."

"The game's crooked?" she said.

"No, it's on the level, but there's a ringer or two, a couple pros to bleed the amateurs dry. It's a massacre in there some nights."

"Why do they keep playing?" Chance said. "The amateurs, I mean."

Stimmer shrugged. "Why do gamblers keep losing? For the thrill. It was too good to last, though. So they're doing one last big game, then shutting it down."

"How do you know all this?" she said. With that level of information, there had to be an inside man. They were always the weakest link, the first to buckle under pressure, give up the rest of the crew in exchange for a deal.

"One of the players. He realized what was going on, got out after the first couple weeks. He told me about it."

"He in this, too?"

"For a finder's fee, that's all. A few grand. I'll take care of that from my end."

"Who are the players?"

"Changes every week, but two or three of them form the core. I have a rough list. I can give it to you, you can check them out yourself. Some old-time Florida guys, a couple Koreans. Every once in a while, some gangsta rapper sits in. All with money to burn, looking to have a little fun, too stupid to know what's going on. Or just don't give a fuck."

"Unprotected?" she said.

"Unprotected, unauthorized, and wide open. No one will get pissed if it gets taken down."

"Except the players," Chance said.

"Most of them will lick their wounds, walk away, write it off," Stimmer said. "The game's illegal anyway. They can't go to the police. And the rest of them . . . well, we'll be a thousand miles away before they even realize what happened."

"Or," Chance said, "if they already suspect the game's crooked, when they get taken off they'll think that's an inside job, too, get mad at the wrong people."

"Could be," Stimmer said and half-smiled. "That's the beauty of it."

"A million plus on the table," she said. "That doesn't sound right."

"That's a best-case scenario. Still, between three people . . ."

"They have a banker there?" she said.

"Yeah. He brings the chips, watches over the money."

"So they'll have some sort of security. Armed."

"There's always a guy with the banker to keep an eye on him, settle any disputes among the players. But it's usually a quiet game. No women, no posses. Just room service food and booze. They come to play."

"You got all this from your inside man?"

"Plus a sketch of the layout. That never changes. Always the same room."

"How do we get in and out?"

"That's what I need you two to help me figure out."

"Your insider," Chance said. "He'll be conspicuously absent when all this goes down, won't he?"

"He hasn't played in a month. He's done with it. He wouldn't mind a little revenge too, for what he lost. He'll be happy with what I give him though. I'll make sure of that."

"What do they play?" she said.

"Hold 'Em, mostly. No limit. Thirty-thousand-dollar buy-in. Sometimes they alternate. Hold 'Em, Omaha, Stud, and Stud Eight. They hire a private dealer for the night."

"How many players?"

"Six to ten," he said. "Since it's the last night, probably the full ten. Some of them will want a chance to win their money back."

"So at least twelve people in there, maybe more."

"Small space, though. Easy to control. We go in heavy, four, five minutes we're out of there."

Chance laced his fingers behind his head, rocked back on his chair.

She thought it over. If Stimmer's information was accurate,

three might be enough. A small crew, but she'd worked with both of them before, knew they were good. It improved the odds.

"You say they're only doing one more game?" she said.

Stimmer nodded. "That's the word."

"When?"

"That's the complication."

"How's that?"

"The timing. It's Sunday."

"Shit," Chance said. "That's just . . ."

"Five days," Stimmer said. "That's all the time we've got."

"I'm unconvinced," she said.

They were in the bar at a Sheraton off the Garden State Parkway, a half hour's drive from the farmhouse. She and Chance had gotten a booth in the back. She had a glass of red wine in front of her, Chance a beer, steaks on the way.

"This was pitched to me as high-end," she said. "Not some half-assed card game."

"I've heard worse."

"You're liking it?"

"I want to know more," he said, "but I didn't hear anything that made me rule it out. Three people, the logistics are simpler. Cut's better, too."

"I don't know." She looked around the bar, scanned faces. "That much money in play at a single game. Hard to buy."

"Look at it this way. Even if it's only half that, it's a good return. If the setup's the way he says it is, all we have to do is go in and grab the bank and skedaddle. Hard to pass that up."

"It always looks easy until you walk in the door."

"Yeah. But like Wayne used to say, 'Plan the work . . .'"

"'. . . and work the plan.' I remember."

The waitress brought their food. For a while, they ate without speaking, comfortable in their silence. It was good to sit across from him, to know he was alive, still on the outside. He was another connection with Wayne, with the way their lives had once been, a reminder of better times. Despite the dangers, the risks of the work, her years with Wayne had been the happiest of her life.

"It made me feel good to see you there," Chance said,

"You don't trust Stimmer?"

"I trust him fine. We've worked together. I value your judgment, though. Knowing you're in makes me feel better."

"I might not be."

"I know. Even if you bail, that tells me something."

"If I do, it doesn't mean the work's wrong. Just that it's not right for me."

"I know. But having you around . . . It's the next thing to having Wayne here, I guess."

"I'm not Wayne."

"No, but you're his partner, *were* his partner."

"Still am."

"That speaks for itself. So how is Daddy Cool?"

"Like I said, one day at a time. He's got a parole hearing coming up."

"How's it look?"

"Hard to tell. We're working on it."

"He was the one schooled me when I needed it," he said. "Kept me out of the joint, out of a box. Taught me how to make it all work. He was good luck for me."

"I know."

"And you were good luck for him."

"Not good enough."

"He always did like to run those long odds. Did pretty well, too, for a long time. He wouldn't have gotten that far without you. Way it played out, nothing you could have done about it."

"I wonder," she said. "Maybe if I'd been with him on that last thing, it would have gone differently."

"Maybe. Or more likely, you'd be inside, too. Some things are just fucked from the start. It's fate. All the planning in the world can't make them come out right."

The waitress came back, and Chance pointed at his empty Sam Adams bottle. She brought another beer, and Chance thanked her with a smile, watched her hips as she walked away.

He looked back at Crissa. "Sorry."

"You been working?" she said.

"Not as much as I'd like to. Nothing good. How about you?"

"On and off. Did something recently. Check-cashing store."

"You slumming?"

"In that case, yeah, way it turned out."

"You've been keeping busy, though."

"Enough."

"So you could bail on this if you wanted to. I might not have that luxury."

"What do you mean?"

"I need it."

"That's a bad way to go into something."

"I know. But you don't always get to choose."

"You're wrong," she said. "You do."

"It's not like I'm desperate. It's just that the last couple things fell apart before they happened. One goddamn thing or another. Bad luck. The kitty's getting hungry."

"Happens."

They sat in silence for a moment.

"Here's what I think," she said. "We go down there, take a look."

"Okay."

"We get a feel for it. Check out the layout. If it looks good, we stay and do it. If not, we walk away."

"That sounds right. When?"

"Soon," she said. "There's something else I need to do first."

EIGHT

The supermarket was closed for the night, metal shutters pulled down over the windows. Only 8:00 P.M., but all the stores on the street were dark.

"Go around back," Eddie said.

Terry pulled the El Camino into the rear lot. There was a loading dock here, an overflowing Dumpster, a pile of flattened cardboard boxes. Three cars: a silver Lexus, a green four-door Mercury, and a white van that said RICHFIELD CONTRACTING on the side.

"How the mighty have fallen," Eddie said.

"This the place? You sure?"

"Yeah, this is it. Pull up alongside the Dumpster, kill the lights. Leave the engine running."

There was a single door by the loading dock, a light in a metal cage above it.

"Should I come in?" Terry said. He'd taken the ring from his eyebrow.

"Hang here. I won't be long. I'm not here to socialize."

He took Casco's gun from his pocket, put it in the glove box, shut it.

"I don't come out in ten minutes," he said, "take that and go in there and start blasting."

Terry looked at him.

"It's a joke," Eddie said. "Stay here. I'll be back in a few minutes."

He got out of the El Camino. The air smelled of garbage. As he neared the door, a motion sensor floodlamp clicked on, bathing him in light. He frowned, tried the door with a gloved hand. It was unlocked.

Inside was a narrow cinder-block hall, tube lights hissing on the ceiling. The smell was in here, too, rotten fruit and vegetables. Voices came from an open door at the end of the hallway. As Eddie neared it, Nicky Conte stepped out.

"There he is, Eddie Santiago. A free man once again."

"Hey, Nicky."

"Good to see you. Come on in."

Inside the cramped office were Tino and a man Eddie didn't know. Tino got up.

"Eddie. So good to see you."

He was skinnier than Eddie remembered, tendons showing in his neck, loose flaps of skin under his jaw. There were liver spots on the backs of his hands.

Eddie took the hug.

"You look well," Tino said. "Strong."

Eddie looked around. A metal desk piled with papers, five dusty closed-circuit TV screens on a wall shelf. One view showed the corridor he'd just come down, another the back lot, the El Camino. The other three looked out on the market's empty aisles.

"Have a seat," Tino said. He motioned to a folding chair. "You know Nick. You met Vincent Rio?"

"No." Eddie nodded at the third man. He was big and blocky, his face pockmarked with acne scars. He wore heavy work boots.

Eddie took the chair. Nicky came in, leaned against the wall.

"How are you, my friend?" Tino said. He sat across from him. "How have you been?"

"Still breathing."

"I hear you. Inside gets tougher as you get older, doesn't it? Believe me, I know."

Eddie shrugged.

"You get settled?" Tino said. "Get a place to stay?"

"Good enough for now."

"Good. Nick, Vincent, can you give us a minute here?"

"Sure," Nicky said. "I want to catch a butt anyway."

"Enough with the smoking," Tino said. "You'll end up like me."

"We'll be out back," Nicky said.

When they were gone, Tino nodded at the door. Eddie rocked back on his chair until he could reach it, pushed it shut with his fingertips.

"How'd those screws treat you inside?" Tino said.

"The usual."

"With respect, though, right?"

"More or less."

"I'm sorry about the confusion with the appeal, the money

and all that. Jew lawyer got his signals crossed. By the time I knew about it, it was too late."

"It's past."

"I know that you, and some of the others, get a little resentful about the plea thing."

"I didn't complain."

"You never do. But you understand that's the way it is, way it should be, right? Nobody with us pleads out, ever. If the government thinks it's got a case, let them prove it in court. Why make it easy for them?"

"I understand."

"That's the way it always was, in the old days. The only way it works. Same rule for everyone. Same for me, same for you."

"I didn't say otherwise."

"I know. I'm just making it clear, in case that was bothering you while you were in. Four years is four years."

"Five," Eddie said.

"Whatever. They want you thinking on it. That's how they get to you."

"No one got to me."

"This last case they threw at me," Tino said. "That bullshit extortion rap. They were talking twenty years."

He touched his chest. "Here I am, sixty-six years old, only one lung. They figured I'd take the five they were offering, be happy about it. I said, 'Fuck you, take me to trial.' And they did and they lost, because it was a bullshit case to start with. That's the way they work, they try to scare you."

Eddie looked at the TV screen. Nicky and Rio were standing outside the back door, smoking cigarettes, looking at the El Camino.

"Who's that you brought with you?" Tino said.

"My partner."

"I know him?"

"Maybe. Terry Trudeau. We celled together in Rahway a few years back. He's a good kid."

"You trust him?"

"You don't need to worry about him."

"You got a place to stay. You need anything else?"

"Work."

"We'll do what we can, get you earning again," Tino said. "A good man is always valuable. And you're the best. That's what I said to Nick. I told him, you can't find a better man than Eddie the Saint. No matter what it is you need done."

Eddie said nothing.

"Got some sad news the other day, though. You hear about our friend Casco?"

"What about him?"

"Someone jumped him in his office, cleaned out the safe. Killed him right there. Two in the back of the head."

"Some junkie probably. They catch who did it?"

"No, not yet. To be honest, I doubt they will. You had some money with him, didn't you?"

"A little. Not much. Guess it's gone now."

"He was a good man, a good friend. He handled a lot of things for me. Made me a lot of money. Whoever killed him did me a disservice."

"You want me to look into it?"

Tino shook his head.

"No need. You just got home, I'm sure you've got other

things on your mind. Besides, what good would it do anyway? He's gone."

"That's right."

On the screen, Nicky and Rio finished their cigarettes, tossed the butts away, came back inside.

"Do me a favor," Tino said. "Open that door. That way they'll know we're finished."

Eddie leaned back, twisted the knob, left the door ajar. Nicky and Rio came back in.

"You got a cell?" Tino said.

"No."

Tino pointed to Nicky, who took a cell phone from his jacket pocket, held it out. Eddie took it.

"My number's already in there," Nicky said. "In case you need to reach me."

Eddie looked at Tino.

"Nick gives me messages," Tino said. "Calling him is like calling me."

"It's prepaid, untraceable," Nicky said. "When it's used up, just toss it. I'll give you another."

Eddie stood. "All right." He put the phone in his coat pocket.

"It's good to see you," Tino said. "Good to have you back." He rose, put a hand on Eddie's shoulder for support, embraced him again.

"We'll talk soon," he said. "Look after yourself. Have some fun. You should be enjoying your freedom."

"I am," Eddie said.

NINE

She hated Texas.

As the 747 swung around on final approach, the lights of San Antonio began to emerge through the thin clouds. Her stomach tightened. She'd spent eighteen years of her life in Texas, spent another fifteen trying to stay out.

She and Wayne had been living in Wilmington, Delaware, when the work had come up, a jewelry wholesaler outside Houston. The middle of February, and she'd been down with the flu, weak and hollow-eyed. She stayed behind when he left.

It was supposed to be a give-up by the owner, the guns for show. Wayne had gone in with Larry Black, a pro from St. Louis they'd worked with before, both of them in Federal Express uniforms. But a clerk with a concealed weapon had gone cowboy in the office, shot Wayne through the shoulder, winged the owner by accident.

Larry Black had gotten Wayne out of there, but two blocks

away their driver misjudged a turn, took out a fire hydrant and park bench, and put himself through the windshield. Larry Black got away, but Wayne and the driver went down for armed robbery and conspiracy, ten to fifteen each. She'd been in the courtroom for the sentencing. He'd flashed a smile at her as they led him away in shackles.

Don't ever work in Texas if you don't have to, he'd told her once. *That's one state it takes too goddamn long to get out of.*

She got her suitcase at baggage claim and walked out of the terminal into dry heat, the night air still and oppressive. She was sweating by the time she reached the rental garage. They gave her a big Chrysler 300, all they had left. She shucked off the leather jacket, settled into the cushioned seat, turned the air conditioner on high.

She'd find a motel in the city tonight, head southeast on 181 tomorrow for the ride down to Kenedy. She knew the route well, made the drive five times a year. Halfway between Poth and Falls City, she'd pass Seven Tears, the town where she'd grown up. She never once had stopped.

The visiting room was decorated for the holidays, tinsel taped to cinder-block walls, an artificial Christmas tree in one corner. She knew the presents below it were just empty boxes in wrapping paper.

Nine thirty in the morning and most of the tables were taken. The visitors were almost all women, the majority black or Mexican, with children in tow. She sat at a table in the far corner, as far from the guards as possible, the same spot she always chose for contact visits. Vending machines hummed. Bright sunlight slanted through the windows onto the checkerboard floor.

The conversations at the tables were quiet, inmates in starched khakis with their hands in view at all times, two guards keeping watch. Cameras on all four walls.

She looked up when the security door buzzed. A guard held it open, and Wayne came out, looked around, saw her, smiled. He limped slightly as he started toward her. His black hair was combed straight back, less of it now, streaked with silver above his ears. She stood.

"Hey, darlin'," he said.

"Hey, babe."

She leaned toward him on impulse, stopped. They were allowed a fifteen-second embrace at the beginning and end of every visit, but he wouldn't do it anymore. It made it too hard to say good-bye, he'd said.

They sat, and he winced as he settled on the bench. She reached across, took his hand. On the inside of his left wrist was a faint blue tattoo, the Chinese character for "perseverance." It was a mirror of the one on her own wrist.

"You look good," he said. "How was the trip?"

"Same as always."

She looked into his dark brown eyes. There were more lines around them this time, more deeply etched.

"You're limping," she said.

"This sciatica is kicking my tired old ass."

"It won't go away by itself. You need treatment."

"Only thing left is an operation, and I'm not letting them do that here. I'll end up in a wheelchair. Or worse."

"They give you anything for it? Painkillers?"

"In here? Doesn't happen, girl."

His khakis were loose, the shirt buttoned high, an inch of white T-shirt visible beneath. She wondered how much weight he'd lost.

"You had me worried," she said. "No letters for a while."

"They're lockdown crazy up in here lately. Three times in the last two months. No phone, and no visits to the commissary for stamps. Not that there's much to write about. Same old, same old, every day."

She squeezed his hand.

"Wasn't expecting to see you again so soon," he said.

"I decided to make the trip."

"You going down to Two Rivers?"

"This afternoon."

"How's she doing?" he said.

"Good, as far as I can tell. Growing up. She turned nine in February."

"She still with your cousin?"

She nodded. "That's her family now." It hurt to say it.

"Maybe someday you can work that out."

"The way I live . . ." she said. "She's better off where she is."

He ran his thumb over her knuckles.

"Sorry," he said. "Guess I shouldn't bring that up."

"I'm doing what's best for her."

"I know. You still up north?"

"For now."

"How you like it?"

"I like it fine. But sometimes I think I'm losing my manners."

"Get used to the cold yet, Texas girl like you?"

"Not a Texas girl anymore."

"I guess not. That's good. You're the smartest thing to ever come out of Seven Tears. And the prettiest."

"That's not saying much."

"You were too big for that town, girl. Hell, you were too big for Texas."

"I talked to Rathka."

"And?"

"He's still working on it. His man in Austin says he needs more up front."

"He's a goddamn thief. How much?"

"Don't worry about that."

"If he's sticking you up, tell him to go fuck himself. I'll take my chances with the board."

"Not good enough. I don't like the odds."

"I won't have you getting robbed by some spit-slick Texas lawyer son of a bitch."

"Let me worry about that. March isn't far away."

"What did you tell Rathka?"

"I told him I'd get it."

"Now hold on with that, I—"

"I'm not gonna sit and watch you rot in here. You'd do the same if the situations were reversed."

He sat back.

"What about that house you told me about?" he said. "The one you wanted to buy?"

"We're still talking. We'll see what happens."

"If it comes down to paying some lawyer or buying that house, you know what you need to do, right?"

"Let me take care of it," she said.

He looked at the nearest guard. He was chewing gum, thumbs hooked in his belt, looking at no one in particular.

Wayne lowered his voice. "How'd things go in Pennsylvania?"

"Not that great." The guard had his back to them now. "But there's something else coming up. Hector put me onto it."

"Too soon."

"Maybe. Maybe not," she said.

"Anyone I know?"

"Stimmer. Chance."

"That it?"

"For now."

"How much exposure?"

"Not much," she said. "Publicly, not at all. Closed doors. Private event."

"Never as easy as it sounds."

"I know."

"Good men, though."

"Stimmer put it together. I'm going to go have a look, make a decision."

"I still think it's too soon."

"Sometimes you have to take the opportunities as they come."

A baby began to cry. He looked over. The mother hushed it in soft Spanish. After a moment, he looked back at Crissa.

"I was thinking," he said.

"About what?"

"You. And that little girl. You ever hear from her father?"

"We've been over this. I expect he's inside. Or dead. Like I told you, we only ran together for a year. Last time I saw him, he was living in a trailer, a needle in his arm most of the time. You saved me from all that, remember?"

"You never did have much luck picking men."

"I didn't do so bad the last time around. What's your point?"

"You should be looking beyond all this is my point. Buy that house for starters. Find a man, settle down. Figure out a way to raise your daughter."

"I've got a man."

"This is no life to live," he said. "And the game is rigged. You see money for a minute—" he gestured around him— "and a place like this for a long time."

"I'll get you out of here. I'm not gonna wait seven years, either."

He turned her hand over, rubbed his thumb along her tattoo. She felt goose bumps rise on her arm, touched her calf to his under the table.

"This is hard to say. But I mean it." He met her eyes. "What you need to do is get on with your life."

"Don't start this again."

"Worry about yourself. And that little girl."

"We've been partners a long time—"

"And most of that, I was in here."

"—and that's an investment. Too much to just give up."

"Sometimes it's the smart thing to do. Cut your losses. Walk away. Ain't nothing in this world getting any younger. Me included."

"You're not old."

"Old enough. Too old for you. And by the time I get out of

here, not much use to anyone. Don't waste your life waiting on me, Red. That would hurt me worse than anything."

He looked over his shoulder, gestured to the guard. This was always the way he ended it, before their time was up. Not letting the moment be decided by someone else.

She stood with him, fingers still entwined in his. The security door buzzed and opened, the guard waiting beside it.

He let go of her hand.

"Keep it between the ditches, Red. And think about what I said."

She pulled the Chrysler to the curb, powered down the window, and looked at the house across the street. Sprinklers spun in the yard, rainbow patterns in the water. The lawn was neatly trimmed, deep green despite the heat. Cutout Christmas decorations in the big front window, Santa Claus with sleigh, a snowman in a top hat, candy canes. A Ford Explorer was in the driveway.

She looked at her watch. One o'clock.

As if on signal, the front door of the house opened, and Maddie bounded down the steps. She wore jeans and a pink T-shirt, her strawberry blond hair braided into pigtails. Only six months since Crissa had last seen her, but she seemed a foot taller. Crissa felt something pull inside her.

Her cousin Leah came out next, wearing a sleeveless T-shirt, her arms toned, black hair cut short, a new look. They'd been close growing up, only a year's difference between them, then gone their separate ways. The week that Leah graduated high school with honors, Crissa was already on the run, in the first of a trio of doomed relationships marked by petty crime and casual violence. She'd taken beatings from those men, thought of it as a kind of love, a sign of the intensity with which they lived the lives they'd chosen, something Leah would never understand. Then she'd met Wayne, and he'd shown her a different world, a different way to live. Nothing had ever been the same again.

As she watched, Leah unlocked the Explorer with a keypad, Maddie climbing up into the passenger side. When Leah got behind the wheel, she looked across at Crissa for a moment, nodded. She nodded back. The Explorer backed out of the driveway.

She followed them a half mile to a playground beside a redbrick community center. As soon as the Explorer pulled to the curb, Maddie was out of it, joining the dozen or so kids shouting and laughing on the slides and swings.

Crissa parked behind the Explorer, shut off the engine, watched Maddie climb the ladder of a yellow plastic slide and pause at the top, a look of concentration on her face. She pushed off, slid down into the sand, ran back around to the ladder.

Leah got out, walked to the Chrysler. "Right on time."

"She's getting big," Crissa said.

"She is that." They watched her go down the slide again. "Got her braces last week. I think she's finally getting used to them."

She handed Crissa a CD in a clear plastic case. "Those pictures you wanted."

"Thanks. I have something for you, too." She tapped the

newspaper on the seat beside her, the manila envelope under it.

Leah looked back at the playground. Maddie was at the whirlaround now, pushing while other kids rode, then hopping on after them.

"She's got a lot of energy," Crissa said.

"Wish I had half of it. It's hard for us to keep up." She nodded at the CD. "Those photos are all new. There's some class pictures, too."

"How's she doing there?"

"Fine. She loves school, loves to read. Always got her nose in a book."

"That's good."

Maddie leaped from the whirlaround while it was in motion, tumbled into the dirt. Leah started toward the playground, and Crissa felt for the door latch. In the next instant, Maddie was up again and laughing, running to climb back on.

Leah came back to the car. "Like I said, she keeps us busy."

"What else does she like to do?"

"Earl takes her fishing up to Belton Lake every once in a while. She loves that. She's the most patient child I've ever known. Good with her little sister, too."

Leah and Earl had given up on having children, had been told they never would. Then, four years after they'd agreed to take Maddie, Leah had gotten pregnant out of the blue, and Jenny had come along.

Crissa folded the newspaper around the envelope, handed it out. "That's an extra five thousand. You can put it toward the dentist bill."

Leah tucked the paper under her arm. Crissa sensed her nervousness. Still scared of you after all this time, she thought. Scared of what you've done. Of what you might do.

"How's that new account working out?" Crissa said.

"No problems. Just like before. Money's in there the first of every month, right on time."

"You need to take some of that, put it to the mortgage or whatever, go ahead."

"We wouldn't do that. That's Maddie's money."

"I'm saying, if you had to, I'd understand."

"I'll tell Earl."

"Where is he?"

"He's got Jenny with him. They're over to the Super S, picking up some groceries. I told him you'd called. Figured it would be better this way, just me and Maddie."

"It bother him when I come down here?"

"I wouldn't know. He doesn't say."

"It bother you?"

Leah didn't answer. She looked to the playground, raised a hand to shade her eyes. Maddie and three other kids were playing tag, racing back and forth.

"You worried I'm going to show up some day," Crissa said, "take her away? You can stop worrying."

"I guess we just wonder what exactly it is you want, coming around the way you do."

"Just to look in on her from time to time. That's all."

From the playground, Maddie yelled, "Mom!"

Crissa looked up.

"One second, honey," Leah called back. "Stay put, I'll be right there." She looked at Crissa. "I have to go."

Crissa watched her go back to the Explorer, put the news-paper inside. Maddie ran to her and wrapped arms around her legs, knocking her back. Leah hoisted her, turned her upside down, dangled her for a moment, Maddie squealing with laughter. Then she set her down and took her hand, and they walked back toward the swings.

Maddie turned, looked back. She's going to ask her mother who that lady is, Crissa thought. And Leah's going to tell her never mind, honey. It's nobody you know.

Maddie climbed on a swing, scuffed her heels in the sand. Leah got behind her to push.

This is what you came all this way to do, Crissa thought. Spy on your own daughter for ten minutes, like some kid-napper. Get a glimpse of the life you can never have.

She started the engine. Leah looked over at her, Maddie swinging high. Crissa nodded at her, pulled away from the curb. She watched them in the rearview until they were out of sight.

On the drive back, the sky grew dark, lightning flashing on the horizon. Soon the rain came pouring down, the traffic slowing. She put her lights and wipers on. Thunder boomed above her, and then she heard the click of hail hitting the car, watched it bounce off the blacktop ahead of her.

It took her almost three hours to get back to San Antonio. She checked into a Best Western south of the city. Her flight was in the morning, so she'd spend the night here, get an early start tomorrow.

She watched television in her room, thunder sounding

outside, but couldn't concentrate. At six, she sprinted through the rain to the restaurant across the parking lot.

Her steak was undercooked, oozed pink when she cut into it. She ate only half, had a second glass of wine after the waitress took her plate away. She watched rain sluice down the big windows, lightning split the dark sky.

Back in the room, exhaustion settled on her, her limbs like lead. She peeled off her wet clothes, climbed into the shower. As the steam rose around her, she closed her eyes, turned her face to the water.

She thought about Maddie on the swing, laughing and running with the other kids, calling for her mother. Thought about Wayne limping back to his cell, the clang of heavy doors shutting behind him.

After a while, she sat in the tub, legs pulled up, arms around them. She lowered her head, the hot water beating down on her, and began to cry.

TEN

The third time they drove past the hotel, Crissa said, "Pull over."

Chance guided the rental Chevy into the parking lot of a seafood restaurant. He drove to the far end of the lot, parked beneath a palm tree.

From this angle, they had a clear view of the hotel across the street, could see the blue of the ocean beyond. Cars sped by on Seabreeze Boulevard. He shut the engine off, powered down his window.

"Here's something I don't like," he said. "Beach in back. Only way out is the front, right into all this." He nodded at the traffic.

She took the digital camera from the floor. "Late enough, it might not be too bad."

Chance sat back to stay out of frame. She raised the viewfinder to her eye, took a shot of the hotel. It was smaller than its neighbors, only twelve stories high, pink stucco. The portico out front read LA PALOMA. A U-shaped driveway curved beneath it, a cluster of palm trees shading the front entrance.

She took more shots, changing the angle each time.

"We'll need to get out on the beach, too," she said. "Get a look at the back."

A red Porsche pulled up in front of the hotel, a valet coming out to meet it. The driver got out, handed his keys over, was greeted by a uniformed doorman. The valet climbed in the car, pulled away, and turned down a ramp into an underground garage.

"Service entrance, left side of the building," Chance said.

She twisted to find the right angle, took a shot of it. It was a recessed doorway semihidden by a concrete wall topped with flowers.

"Someone will need to take a look down there," she said. "See what the setup is."

"I might could do that."

She tracked up the front of the hotel, the rows of windows, some with curtains drawn. Each room had a balcony, a sliding glass door. She took more shots.

It was almost dusk, the sky behind the hotel darkening to a deeper blue. A spotlight hidden in the palms out front flickered on, bathed the face of the hotel in pale blue light.

"The balconies," she said.

"What about them?"

"If the beach side is the same, that's the way we'll go in."

"How do we get up there?"

She lowered the camera. "Rappel maybe."

"From the roof?"

"Or another balcony."

"Hold on, no one said anything about that."

"You scared of heights?"

"Scared of falling from them."

"It's no big deal," she said. "A half hour's practice with the equipment and you'll be fine."

"How do you know so much about it?"

"Rock climbing. This will be easy compared to that."

The valet came back up the ramp, sat in a folding chair by the front entrance.

"I used to do that," Chance said.

"What?"

"Valet. At a high-rise condo in Seattle. I was nineteen. Wore a uniform and everything. It was a good gig, lots of tips. Then a resident caught me smoking a joint in the parking garage one night, got me fired."

"Too bad."

"Not really. I kept my uniform. A month later, I came back with a guy I knew. Middle of the night, we went in with masks, tied the valet and doorman up. For the next two hours, I stood outside in my uniform. Every car that came in, I drove two blocks away and onto a car carrier parked on a side street. Porsches, BMWs, Mercedes, a 'Vette. By the afternoon they were all on a container ship headed for Kuwait. I made a lot of money that night."

"Pretty ambitious for a nineteen-year-old."

"I had my moments."

Darker now, stars showing in the blackness over the ocean. A worker in a blue jumpsuit with NBS MAINTENANCE stitched on the back came out of the service entrance, lit the row of tiki torches that lined the driveway. Oily smoke drifted up.

"Get some shots of that uniform," Chance said.

She squinted through the viewfinder in the fading light, shot until the worker went back in the building, then lowered the camera.

"So far," she said, "it's just the way he told us."

"It is."

"So what do you think?"

"It's doable."

"In that time frame?"

"Maybe. If we can figure out a way to get in that doesn't include me climbing down the side of a building."

They watched as another car pulled up in front of the hotel, the valet springing up to meet it.

"So tell me something," Chance said.

"What?"

"What do you do with your money? I mean, when you work."

"Lots of things."

"Like what?"

"Construction projects. Strip malls. There are always people looking for loose cash to sink into an investment, give you a return on it you can legitimately claim."

"You pay taxes?"

"Every year. You don't?"

He looked at the hotel, shook his head. "I'm off the grid."

"You think you are," she said. "Until they nail you."

"I'm good so far."

"Makes me wonder if it's all worth it, though."

"What?"

"The money. What we get for what we do, the risks we take. How it balances out. Or doesn't."

"Beats working in a factory," he said. "I've done that, too. You watch your life blow by you every day. And the days you're not working, you're too friggin' tired to enjoy anyway. You say you saw Wayne?"

"Two days ago." She'd flown from San Antonio to New York, then taken Amtrak to Florida.

"How's he making out?"

"Hard to tell. He doesn't talk much about what goes on inside."

"Doesn't want to worry you."

"Maybe."

She took shots of the boulevard, north and south. The light was all but gone now. She lowered the camera.

"Let's find a Kinko's or something, print these out," she said. "Then go see Stimmer."

He started the engine. "So, what are you thinking?"

"I'm thinking," she said, "that it's a go."

Stimmer laid the guns out on the coffee table, a Glock 9 mm, a Browning automatic, and a short-barreled MP5 machine pistol. She picked up the Glock, turned it over in her hand, felt its weight.

They were in a bungalow Stimmer had rented a few miles west of the city, in a neighborhood of dead lawns and single-story stucco homes marked with gang graffiti. The living room furniture was a battered couch and cheap table, a pair of metal folding chairs. An open door led into the single bedroom. She had the couch, Stimmer and Chance the chairs. Paper printouts of the hotel shots were on the table.

"What's with the grease gun?" Chance said. "You looking to clear a room?"

"It's psychological," Stimmer said. He wore a sleeveless T-shirt and cargo shorts. There was a fanged skull tattoo on his upper arm, an elaborate crucifix on his calf.

He picked up the MP5, extended the metal tube stock, locked it into place.

"Weapon like this gets people's attention. Lets them know you're serious. That's what we want, right? What do they call it? 'The illusion of imminent death'?"

The house smelled of mildew and rotted fruit, the jalousied windows covered by dirty pull shades. She wondered how he slept in here. A palmetto bug scuttled across the linoleum in the kitchen, disappeared beneath the refrigerator.

"I bought all of these down here," Stimmer said. "They go right into a canal when we're done."

She set the Glock back down. "I put together a list of what I think we'll need," she said. She tapped a printout. "We were looking at those balconies."

"So was I," Stimmer said. He laid the MP5 across his lap. "The room with the game is on the beachside, 1102. The balconies are wider there, better for us. There's no way we're getting in the front door of that room while the game's going on."

"We'll need to figure a way to get through that sliding glass door," she said.

"Not an issue. No one smokes in the room, they have to go outside. So they leave the door unlocked."

"We'll need rappelling equipment for two people. Can you swing that?"

"Shouldn't be a problem. I'll take care of it tomorrow."

"Black jumpsuits for two of us," she said. "A blue one for the third. We have to fake some stitching on the back, name of a maintenance company. Doesn't have to be perfect, just enough to pass casual inspection."

Stimmer nodded. "Masks and gloves, too. I can do all of that."

"About this rappel thing," Chance said. "I don't know if I'm down with that."

"You don't need to be," Stimmer said. "I've done it. All you'll have to do is help organize the equipment up top, watch the safety lines."

"That's better."

"We need someone to take a look inside," she said. "Maybe get some pictures."

"I've been in there," Stimmer said. "Couple weeks back. I stayed there one night, walked around the place. Eleventh floor, too."

"Sure that was smart?" she said.

"I used another name and credit card. Nothing to worry about. Eleven-oh-two is at the end of the hall, north side. I was in 904, two floors down and one room over. Layout's probably the same. I sketched it all out."

"Good," she said.

"If it's different, we'll play it by ear when we get in there. Players start arriving about nine, but the game doesn't pick up speed until midnight or so. I figure we go in around one. Too early for people to start dropping out, but late enough that they're starting to get tired. Easier to handle."

"That sounds right," she said.

"Now, on every hall there's a maintenance closet," he said. "Locked, but easy to pick. Each one has a trash chute that goes down to the basement, directly off the garage. That way we don't have to carry anything downstairs. We pack it all into a pair of duffels—money, guns, masks, everything— dump them into the chute. We walk away clean, just in case we're stopped. Then we meet up in the basement, pick up the bags, and get gone."

"How do we get into the basement?" Chance said.

"It's a maintenance shop as well, open during the day. I was able to get a look inside. There's tools in there, so they lock the door at night, but it'll be easy to get through. No alarm. There's a reserved parking spot in the garage, right outside the door, for the maintenance company van. They're independent contractors, only there during business hours or emergencies. I got a couple shots of their vehicle."

"So we'll need a van?" Chance said.

"I got that covered. The van's old, white. Easy to match. I found one like it over in Davie, bought it for five hundred cash. They'll keep it there until I pick it up. We'll need to do a paint job on the side, re-create the logo, but we've got the pictures to match it against."

"So who's paying for all this?" Crissa said.

"I am, so far," Stimmer said. "Afterward we'll do a normal split. Expenses off the top, then a three-way divide."

"What about your inside guy?" she said.

"That comes out of my share. I'll take care of him."

Or maybe he'll end up in a canal, too, she thought. Stimmer seemed the type. Cheaper than paying him, and one less loose end. In the long run, though, it was a bad way to do business. Bodies had a way of turning up, and greed and paranoia could ruin the best of plans.

"We'll have another car parked nearby," Stimmer said. "We roll out of there in the van, split up when we reach the car. Whoever's driving the van takes the equipment and the money. Then we meet up later, here."

He nodded at the Glock. "You want to take that now?"

She shook her head. "Night of. We'll leave everything here until we're ready."

"Fine with me," he said.

"I think we're done here," she said. "We'll meet tomorrow, get the equipment sorted out, run through everything again. We don't have much time."

"That's an understatement," Chance said. "One day to get ready. Can we even make that work?"

"We will," she said.

Chance dropped her at her hotel in Deerfield Beach. She went up to the room and got the disc Leah had given her, then let herself into the hotel's business center with her key card. The room was empty, the three computers and fax machine shut down for the night.

She sat at a terminal, powered it up, and slid the disc in.

There were twelve photos on it, all recent. Maddie at a swimming pool, water wings on her arms, splashing. Another on the front lawn of the house, Maddie crouched and smiling up at the camera. In the next, she was blowing out candles on a birthday cake, Jenny beside her. Then a class portrait on the school steps. The bottom of the photo read GRADE FIVE — ELKTAIL ELEMENTARY SCHOOL — TWO RIVERS, TEXAS — 2011.

She clicked through all the pictures twice, with that same pull inside she'd felt at the playground. You're a beautiful little girl, she thought. But you're not really mine anymore, are you?

This was a mistake, she realized. She should have waited until she got home to look at the photos, when the work was over. Right now she needed her edge, needed to be cold, smart. No tears.

She ejected the disc, punched the power button, watched the screen fade to black.

ELEVEN

She rode the elevator to the tenth floor, then got out and took the stairs. At the top, a fire door said NO ADMITTANCE. She pushed through, went up the short flight of stairs to the roof.

She'd come in the front door with a group of drunk conventioneers, joined them in the elevator. The doorman hadn't seemed to notice her. The conventioneers had gotten off at the fifth floor, gone noisily to their rooms, left her alone.

She opened the roof door and stepped out into the night. In front of her was the immense blackness of the ocean, the moon a glow behind clouds.

Stimmer and Chance were waiting in the lee of the big air-conditioning unit, sitting with their backs against it. They'd arrived an hour apart, Stimmer first, Chance dropping him off, then coming back with the van. She'd taken a cab, had it leave her four blocks away at another hotel, then walked here.

The air conditioner rattled and thrummed, the only sound up here besides the wind. Heat lightning pulsed on the horizon.

They got to their feet when they saw her. Stimmer was already in his jumpsuit, Chance in the maintenance uniform, both wearing gloves. Chance opened a duffel bag, began to draw equipment out.

The blacktop was warm through her sneakers—residual heat from the day. She looked around. On both sides were more hotels, a long curve of them following the beach. To the front, traffic moved on Seabreeze. The far right lane emptied onto the bridge that spanned the Intracoastal Waterway and led to the city proper.

Chance held out her jumpsuit. She pulled it on over her jeans and T-shirt, a tight fit, zipped it. There was a Velcroed pocket on each side, big enough for a weapon. Chance handed her the Glock. She checked it, slipped it into the right pocket, smoothed it shut. The bundle of plasticuffs he gave her went into the other pocket.

Stimmer had two nylon ropes anchored around the air-conditioning unit, was pulling on them to test them. Chance held up one of the harnesses for her. She stepped into it, tightened the belt, tugged on the leather rappel gloves he gave her.

Stimmer drew the MP5 from the duffel, the stock retracted. He'd jury-rigged a harness on his back for it, strapped it in place. Chance helped him into the rappel gear.

They got busy with the lines, feeding them through the carabiners and belay devices. She double-checked hers, tugged on the rope to test it. She gave Stimmer the thumbs-up.

A gust of wind blew in from the ocean, lifted grit from the rooftop, swirled it in the air. It was stronger than they'd expected. They'd have to take it into account when they went over the side.

She paid out rope, walking backward to the roof edge. She turned, looked down, felt a hollowness in her stomach. Thirteen floors below was the concrete patio, the blue light of the swimming pool, closed for the night, a stack of plastic chairs beside it. Beyond the patio, the empty beach. Light came through the ground-floor windows, illuminated a brief stretch of sand.

If the rigging failed, she'd have two choices. Push away and hope she cleared the patio and hit the sand, or angle in and try to make the pool. Either way, she knew, the fall would probably kill her.

"You ready?" Stimmer said. She nodded. He pulled on a black ski mask, handed her another. She tugged it down over her face, adjusted the eye holes. She tried to swallow, couldn't gather enough saliva.

She repositioned herself, looked down again. Directly below was the dark shape of an unlit balcony—1202. They knew it was vacant, had called the room twice tonight to be sure. Below that, the balcony of 1102, the flagstones faintly illuminated by light coming through a sliding glass door.

Chance was by the air-conditioning unit, checking the rigging. He gave her the thumbs-up. She hitched the harness to a more comfortable position, leaned back until the line grew taut. Then she stepped backward over the edge, planted her feet against the stucco wall.

She played out rope, the nylon stretching as it took her

weight. Her right hand worked the belaying device at her hip. Don't look down and don't look up, she thought. Concentrate on what you're doing.

She lowered herself, testing the tension, letting the rope out in increments through the cinch links, her sneakers scuffing on the wall. She juddered in stages down the side of the building, the wind pushing gently against her. She felt exposed, waited for someone on the ground to see her, cry out.

She let out more rope, and then suddenly the first balcony was under her. The wind blew her toward the building. She braced her feet on the wrought-iron railing, let it take her weight. Three seconds of rest and then she let out more line, pushed away. She could hear the ocean.

Stretched across the railing, the line held her farther out from the building now. She looked down, saw the balcony of 1102 just a few feet below. More line, and then she swung her weight out—once, twice—let the momentum carry her back in, her legs extended. On the third try, she hooked the railing with her feet, pulled herself in. Then she played out a final three feet of rope, swung her hips over the railing, and landed soft on the balcony.

She crouched there, not breathing. The sliding glass door was open two inches, the breeze stirring the curtain inside. The room beyond was half-lit. A wind chime sounded from another balcony.

She put a hand on the flagstones for balance, used the other to undo the harness. She eased out of it, then double-knotted the trailing line around one of the carabiners.

Movement above her. She looked up, saw Stimmer coming down. He tried to swing in to the balcony, missed. She caught his ankle on the second try, guided him in. His feet touched the flagstones, and she pulled him down beside her.

They waited, listening. He eased his harness off, knotted the line, tugged twice. The two harnesses rose off the flagstones, brushed once against the railing, and were gone.

She looked at the door, remembering the layout Stimmer had sketched. The living room here, then the dining room beyond, where the game was. To the left, a bedroom where the bank would be. The living room was big. They would have to cross it fast and silent.

Stimmer had the MP5 free, was cradling it in his arms. Clouds parted and the moon brightened. She put a hand on his shoulder to hold him there. They waited, heard the distant rumble of thunder out over the ocean.

When the clouds closed again, she crawled across the flagstones. She took out the Glock, used her other hand to hook the lip of the door. It moved smoothly as she pushed. Cool air flowed out. Wind billowed the curtain.

She could hear voices now, terse statements punctuated by silence. She got to her feet, Stimmer rising beside her. She eased the curtain aside.

When she stepped into the living room, there was a small white-haired man coming toward them, an unlit cigar in his mouth. She aimed the Glock at him, touched an index finger to her lips. Stimmer moved to her right, the MP5 up. The old man looked at them without fear, said nothing.

Light spilled from the dining room, but she and Stimmer stood in shadow. She pointed at the man with her left hand, made a circular motion. He took the cigar from his mouth, looked at both of them, then turned and began to walk back. They followed him.

When he stepped into the dining room, he looked at the nine men at the table and said, "Bad news."

TWELVE

"Sit down," Stimmer told the old man. He moved to the head of the table to cover them all, the MP5's stock extended now. "This is a robbery. Don't make it a murder."

The old man took his chair. Crissa pointed the Glock into the room. Ten men at the table, one of them in vest and tuxedo shirt, a deck of cards in his hand. The dealer. Green felt cloth on the table, a pile of multicolored chips in the center, more stacked in front of each player. Against the wall, a table full of room service food, silver trays and liquor bottles, a coffeepot.

She felt their eyes on her as she moved past, into the corridor. A big man in a Hawaiian shirt was coming out of the bedroom, the door half open behind him. She aimed the Glock at his face. He stopped, looked at her, the gun, raised his hands to shoulder height.

There was a TV on in the bedroom behind him. In the

hall, a big tank full of bright tropical fish bubbled softly. Those were the only sounds.

"Ricky," the old man called from the dining room. "Do as they say. It's all right."

She pointed at the floor. Ricky sank slowly to his knees on the carpet, hands still up.

"All the way," she said.

He stretched out on his stomach. She straddled him, halffacing the bedroom doorway, reached beneath his shirt, felt the automatic in the clip holster. She pulled it out, patted him down again, took a BlackBerry off his other hip. She dropped both in the fish tank.

"Stay there," she told him and went into the bedroom.

Inside, a bald man in a suit was cramming stacks of bills into a steel attaché case on a table. Beside the case was a teak box of chips.

She tapped the Glock on the door frame to get his attention. He froze, didn't turn.

"Step away from that case," she said.

He raised his hands.

"Back up. That's good. Now kneel."

She crouched behind him, took a walnut-grip .38 from his hip, tossed it on the bed. She pulled a cell phone from his jacket pocket, dropped it beside the gun.

"Facedown," she said. She pushed the Glock into her pocket to free her hands, took out a pair of plasticuffs. He crossed his wrists behind him, and she slipped the cuffs on, drew them tight.

"Stay quiet," she said. "Or I'll gag you."

She took the gun and phone, went back into the hall, dropped them in the tank. Fish jetted away in irritation.

Ricky hadn't moved. She took out another pair of cuffs, bound his hands behind him. He grunted as she tightened them.

She went down the hall to a mirrored foyer, tapped lightly at the front door. When the answering knock came, she worked the locks, opened the door. Chance came in carrying a duffel bag, the ski mask pushed up on his head. The bag clanked as he set it down. She shut the door behind him, and he pulled the mask over his face, adjusted it.

She pointed at the bedroom door. He nodded, drew a folded canvas bag from his jumpsuit.

Back in the dining room, Stimmer stood as before, the MP5 unwavering. The men at the table turned to look at her. Two were Asians in resort wear. Across the table from them sat a young, slim man in a red and white cowboy shirt with pearl snaps. To his left, a heavy man with a pockmarked face, black and silver hair slicked back. He wore a suit jacket, his white shirt open to show a gold Italian horn on a chain. The stack of chips in front of him was the smallest on the table.

"Everybody stay calm," the old man said. "Let them take what they want."

"Sam," said a man in shirtsleeves and thick glasses. "What is this bullshit?"

"Easy, Morrie," the old man said. "Everybody take it easy."

"Gentlemen," Stimmer said. "Wallets and cell phones. On the table."

A groan came up. Sam put the unlit cigar back in his

mouth, then pulled a thick leather wallet from his back pocket, tossed it onto the chips in the center of the table. "No cell phone," he said. "Hate 'em."

Onc by one, the others added wallets and phones to the pile. The heavy man didn't move.

Stimmer came around behind the Asians, faced the heavy man across the table. He leveled the MP5 at his chest.

"Do it," Stimmer said. The heavy man met his eyes.

"Lou," Sam said. "Come on, don't fuck around."

Crissa raised the Glock. "Do what he says." It was taking too long. They were losing the element of surprise, giving the players time to think.

After a moment, Lou said, "Punks." He took a leather billfold from an inside pocket, tossed it with the others, sat back.

"Phone," Stimmer said.

Lou looked at him, then took a thin black cell from another pocket, dropped it on the table.

"Morrie," Stimmer said, looking at the man in glasses. "Take the cash out of those wallets, pile it on the table."

"Why me?"

Stimmer pointed the MP5 at him. Morrie sighed, stood. Stimmer aimed at Lou again, their eyes locked on each other.

Morrie began pulling cash from wallets, dropping it on the table.

"Make sure you get it all," Stimmer said. "Then sit down."

Chance gave a short whistle from the corridor. She went out, saw him with the laundry bag between his feet, one end now bulky with cash. He'd taken Ricky into the bedroom, laid him down next to the banker.

Chance gave her a thumbs-up. *Got it all.* She cocked her

head at the dining room. He nodded, went through. She went around the suite looking for room phones, found three. She unplugged the jack cords at both ends, shoved them into her pocket.

Back in the dining room, Chance was shoveling loose cash and cell phones into the laundry bag, the men watching him. He pulled the drawstring tight and hefted the bag, and she went with him to the front door. She caught a glimpse of herself in the mirrored wall, a masked figure in black.

Chance took the second duffel, pulled it open, the rappelling gear inside. She ejected the magazine from the Glock, cleared the chamber, dropped gun and clip into the bag. Then she stripped out of the jumpsuit, stuffed it in after them. She was pulling at the mask when they heard the flat *crack* of the gunshot.

She looked at Chance. From the dining room, someone said, "Oh good Jesus Christ, no."

She tugged the mask back down, swung around the corner into the dining room. The men had all pushed back from the table, some with their hands up. Gunsmoke hung in the air.

"Oh, Jesus," the man in the cowboy shirt said. "Oh good Jesus Christ."

Lou was sprawled back in his chair, the top of it wedged against the wall behind him, keeping him from falling. There was a black hole on the left side of his chest, the shirt blooming red around it. There was blood on the wall, on the felt, specks of it on the face of the man in the cowboy shirt. Lou slid lower in his seat, eyes half closed.

Silence in the room. She looked at Stimmer. He had the

MP5 to his shoulder. A wisp of smoke drifted up from the breach. No one moved.

"He was reaching for something," Stimmer said.

Lou tumbled slow to the left, out of the chair. The cowboy pulled away, let him fall. He took the chair down with him, thudded onto the floor, and lay still.

Stimmer tracked the gun over the rest of them. The cowboy raised a hand in front of his face. The Asians looked at Stimmer, patient. Sam had his hands up. No one looked at the body.

"Anyone tries to follow us gets the same," Stimmer said.

She turned, moved quick into the hallway. Chance looked a question at her.

"It's fucked," she said. "We need to get out of here."

He held the duffel open. She pulled off her mask, dropped it in. Stimmer came hurrying out of the dining room behind her. He engaged the safety on the MP5, closed the stock, slipped the gun into the bag, started to unzip his jumpsuit.

She didn't wait. She opened the door, looked both ways. The hallway was empty. She stepped out, walked toward the stairwell, turning her face from the cameras, fighting the impulse to run. She passed the maintenance closet, the door propped open as Chance had left it.

On the ninth floor, she left the stairwell, went down the quiet hall to the elevators. She pushed the button, waited, heard the machinery inside. After a few seconds the door on her right opened. Empty. She got in, pushed G.

When the doors opened, she stepped out into the garage. To the left, the door to the maintenance area was propped open with a brick. The van that said NBS MAINTENANCE on the side was parked in a spot near the elevator, nose out. She considered walking past it, up the ramp and onto the street, but she didn't know the area, would be lost around here on foot.

The passenger door was unlocked. She climbed up, leaned over, and turned the key in the ignition. The engine caught. It would save a few seconds. She pushed her glove back from her watch: 2:00 A.M. She looked back at the stairwell, kept a hand on the door latch, ready to pull it, do a runner if she had to.

A few minutes later, the stairwell entrance opened, and Chance and Stimmer came out, Stimmer back in street clothes, unmasked. They went through the maintenance door, and seconds later came out, Stimmer with the duffel, Chance with the laundry bag. They were breathing heavy from the walk down.

Stimmer pulled open the side door of the van, tossed the bags in, climbed in after them, slid the door shut. Chance got behind the wheel, his face white, pulled out of the spot without a word. She ducked below the dashboard as he drove up the ramp, turned left on Seabreeze and past the hotel. She stayed low as the van turned again, then a third time, the tires rumbling over metal plates, the bridge that led to the city itself.

On Los Olas Boulevard, she heard sirens, raised her head far enough to see a police cruiser streaking toward them from the opposite direction, lights flashing. It passed them, headed toward the beach.

They rode for another five minutes, making turns; then she heard tires on gravel, and the van came to an abrupt stop.

She looked out, saw they were in a warehouse parking lot. Stimmer's switch car, a gray Kia, was parked beside a Dumpster.

"Go on," Chance said. "I need to get rid of this thing."

She opened the door, got down, looked around the lot. A dark street, a long row of warehouses on both sides. She heard the side door open behind her, Stimmer getting out, shutting it. Chance pulled away, steered out of the lot.

"Give me the keys," she said.

Stimmer looked at her.

"What?"

"Give me the keys. I'm driving."

After a moment, he shrugged. "Whatever you say."

He took the keys from his pants pocket, tossed them. She caught them in front of her face.

"Let's go," he said.

She got behind the wheel of the Kia, started the engine. He climbed in beside her, didn't speak.

It was a twenty-minute drive to the bus station. There was a trio of taxis waiting at the curb. She drove past them, turned down a side street of darkened businesses, pulled to the curb.

"You'll want to scrub your hands and wrists," she said. "For powder residue. Even with the gloves." It was the first she'd spoken.

"I will," he said. He turned to her. "He was reaching for something. I had to do it."

She nodded, turned the engine off, looked at him.

"What?" he said.

She hit him high in the left temple with her right fist, knocked his head back against the window. He grabbed at her, and she hit him again, a snapping backhand blow with her fist. He lunged across the seat, trying to get atop her, pin her hands. She put a gloved thumb in his eye.

He cried out, backed away against the door, a hand to his face.

"Jesus Christ!" he said. "What the fuck is wrong with you?"

She opened the door, got out. He was still leaning against the passenger door, hand at his eye. Blood dripped from a nostril.

"You'll hear from us," she said and shut the door, headed for the taxi stand. She didn't look back.

THIRTEEN

Chance upended the duffel, dumped the cash out on the hotel bed. Most of it was banded. The banker had been neat.

He shook out the last of the loose bills, and they divided the money into two piles. They counted without speaking, Chance using a pocket calculator, Crissa doing it all in her head. She wore rubber bands on her wrist, slid one off to bind the bills whenever she reached a round number.

When they were done, they counted once more and compared figures. The total came to $418,320.

"Far cry from a million," she said, "but not bad."

It was 4:00 A.M. She was running on adrenaline, would stay awake, catch an 8:10 Amtrak north.

"Any trouble with the guns?" she said.

"I took the MP5 apart before I dumped it. The pieces went into three different canals. The cell phones, too. Fucking Stimmer."

She went through the money again, making three piles this time.

"That's one hundred and thirty-nine thousand, four hundred and forty each," she said. "Before expenses."

"Fuck that. Let him take the expenses out of his share."

"All right."

"Be even better if we cut him out entirely. He deserves it."

"I know. But we're not going to."

"Why not? That son of a bitch almost walked us both into a felony murder rap."

"I'm as pissed as you are," she said, "but if we give him his split, then he takes off, gets clear of here. Otherwise, he hangs around and runs the risk of getting caught, or comes after us looking for his money. Either way, he's a loose end."

"There's another way to solve it."

She shook her head. "No time. We'll both be out of here by morning. Florida is the last place we want to be right now."

She looked at her watch. "Call Stimmer. Tell him we're on our way. I want to get this settled and get out of here. You still in your hotel?"

"I checked out already. My stuff's in the car. I'm ready to roll."

"Good." She opened her suitcase on the other bed, began rolling cash into clothes and underwear, packing them back again. When she closed the lid, she had to press on it to lock it.

"Okay," she said. "Let's go see him."

They drove past the bungalow twice. The blue pickup Stimmer was using was parked in the carport, lit by a single light over a side door. The yard was overgrown with palm trees and bamboo, the house half hidden. Light came through a jalousied front window.

"Find someplace to park, out of sight," she said. "Couple of white people driving around this neighborhood this hour, cops'll think we're trying to score, pull us over."

He found a spot a block away, an overgrown lot beside a boarded-up house. He killed the lights and engine.

"I should come in with you," he said.

She shook her head. Stimmer's share of the money was in a canvas knapsack at her feet.

"I don't want any drama," she said. "I'm going to give him the cash and leave. Way we left it, he'll be happy to see me at all. I'll meet you back here."

"If you're not back in fifteen minutes?"

"Do whatever you think is right. But if I were you, I'd get out of here."

She hefted the knapsack, opened the door, and got out. A soft breeze stirred the trees. It was dead quiet, moonlight filtering through the clouds. She made her way down the street, staying in the shadows, away from the streetlights.

At the bungalow, she stood beside the front window, looked around the edge of the blind. Stimmer was in there alone, sitting on the couch, wearing a white muscle T-shirt, his head in his hands.

She moved to the carport, checked the truck. The cab was empty. Nothing in the bed except a tire iron and a length of chain.

The top panes on the jalousied side door were open and screenless. She tapped the frame twice. Insects buzzed around the light. A lizard scurried across the stucco wall.

Stimmer loomed up on the other side of the glass. He peered out at her, then undid the locks, opened the door.

"Hey," he said. "Come on in."

There was a wedge of cotton in his left nostril, distorting his nose. His right eye was bloodshot. He locked the door again.

She looked around the kitchen. On the counter was a can of Comet and a washcloth.

"You scrubbed your hands," she said. "That's good."

He went past her into the living room, sat heavily on the couch. He leaned forward, his elbows on his knees, looked up at her.

"I don't know what got into me. I panicked. I thought he had a gun."

She set the knapsack on the coffee table.

"Your third," she said. "Just shy of a hundred and forty K. We decided the expenses come out of your share, given the circumstances."

"I fucked up," he said. "I know. I'm sorry." It was hot in there, and she could smell him, a thick, almost animal odor. Adrenaline and sweat.

"I don't like getting caught in the middle of someone else's drama," she said. "Having a lot of planning go to waste because someone lost their shit."

"I understand. I don't know what to say."

"Nothing to say. There's your money."

He got up, went past her into the kitchen.

"I hate to leave it like this," he said. "Let me get you something. A beer. Some water."

"I'll be going."

He opened the refrigerator, took out a bottle of Heineken, twisted the top off.

"Remember to wipe this place down for fingerprints before you leave," she said. "Everything."

"I will. Where's Chance?" He sipped beer, the refrigerator still open.

"See you around," she said, and started for the door.

"Wait a second."

When she turned, he had the beer in his left hand, a black automatic in his right. He pointed it at her.

"Best-laid plans, huh?" he said. "What's that you always say? 'Nothing for it'?"

He put the bottle on the counter.

"Don't be stupid," she said. "Don't make things worse."

She reached for the doorknob. He cocked the gun.

"Where is he?"

She met his eyes.

"You're not half as tough as you think you are," he said. "I put a bullet through your knee, that money's not going to seem so important."

Stay calm, she thought, feeling foolish, angry she had walked into this, let it happen. A mistake Wayne would never have made.

"I'm guessing he's somewhere nearby," Stimmer said. "Looking at his watch. If I keep you here long enough, he'll come looking for you. Even quicker if he hears shots. One way or another, I'll get that money."

She looked at the gun, then at his eyes. He lowered the muzzle to her crotch.

"I could start there," he said. "See how that feels. This thing doesn't make much noise, and in this neighborhood, no one would give a shit anyway."

He shut the refrigerator door. "I'm guessing you two were getting ready to book. Probably as soon as you settled up with me. So odds are he's got the rest of the money with him, right?"

"Wrong."

"If it's not here, it's close. We can cut a deal. You for the money. Come back inside, sit down. Let's talk."

She didn't move. He pointed the gun at her forehead.

"You want it this way, Crissa, that's the way it'll be. I'll put you down right here, wait for Chance to show up, then start all over with him."

If he was going to kill you, he would have done it already, she thought. He won't do anything until he gets the money.

"Go on," he said. He cocked his head at the living room.

"He won't go for it," she said. "No reason to. He's probably miles away from here already." Wondering if it was true.

"I bet not. Go on, sit down."

He backed away, kept the gun on her as she went past. She moved around the coffee table and sat on the couch, looked around. The louvered panes in the front door were closed tight, the door bolted and chained. All the blinds were drawn.

He followed her in, plucked the bloody cotton from his nostril, flicked it at her face. She batted it away.

"I ought to do you right now," he said. "For putting your hands on me like that."

A tiny lizard ran from beneath the couch, crossed the room, and disappeared under the bedroom door. Stimmer stepped back so he had an angle on both the front and side doors. The gun was still pointed at her.

"How long should we give him?" he said.

"He's not coming."

"Then take a good look around this room. It's the last one you'll ever see. Because if I—"

The side door exploded, glass flying in. Something hit the floor and slid along it. The tire iron.

Stimmer turned, pointing the gun at the door, and she kicked the table with both heels, sent it into his shins, knocking him off balance. The gun went off, the shot punching a hole in the side of the refrigerator. She bent, grabbed the table legs, lifted it like a shield and barreled into him, putting her weight behind it. She kept her head down, drove him hard across the room and into the wall, heard the breath go out of him.

The gun fell to the floor. She kicked at it, missed. The front door rattled in its frame, panes of glass falling in to break on the floor.

Stimmer shoved back hard, and she let the table fall, bent for the gun. He swung at her, caught the side of her jaw, and she fell back, landed on top of the gun. She got her legs up to kick at him, and he grabbed her calf, twisted hard, then fell on her with all his weight, drove the breath from her.

Behind him, she saw the front door fly open, the chain broken, Chance coming in.

Stimmer caught her throat with one hand, cocked the other

back to hit her. His eyes were wild. She drove the heel of her right hand into his nose, snapped his head back, and then Chance was looming over them, swinging something. Stimmer went over with a soft "Ugh," his weight coming off her. She kicked him away, scrambled across the floor, got to her feet.

"You okay?" Chance said. He had a foot on Stimmer's back, pinning him there. A leather slapjack dangled from his hand. Stimmer wasn't moving.

"Yeah." Her legs were unsteady, and the left side of her face was numb. She touched it, and pain jetted through her jaw.

Chance bent, picked up Stimmer's gun. He stuck the slapjack in a hip pocket, checked the gun, then aimed it at the back of Stimmer's head.

"Don't," she said.

He looked at her. Stimmer groaned.

"Not here," she said.

"Why not?"

"We can't leave the body here, and we won't have time to get rid of it."

"Same canals I put the guns in."

"No time."

He took the gun away. "We can't just leave him like this."

"We don't need to kill him. Just slow him down, give him something to think about."

He stuck the gun in his belt, got his keys out, and tossed them to her.

"Go get the car, bring it around front," he said. "I'll handle it."

He took the slapjack back out, looked down at Stimmer, and then bent over him. His arm rose and fell. Stimmer groaned again, then went silent.

She picked up the knapsack, went out the front door. Behind her, she could hear the sound of weighted leather on flesh. Chance grunting with each blow, Stimmer not making any noise at all.

She waited with the lights off, the engine running. Chance came out of the darkness of the side yard, opened the passenger door, and got in. She pulled away.

"How'd you leave him?" she said.

"He won't walk too well for a while. And I did his ribs pretty good. He could die from that, I guess, if we're lucky."

To the east, dawn was a red glow on the horizon.

"Find a bridge somewhere," he said. "I need to get rid of this gun and the slapjack. And we should whack up the rest of that money."

"That'll be simple," she said. "Sixty-nine thousand, seven hundred and twenty each." That would bring her split to $209,160.

"What time's your train?" he said.

"Eight ten."

"No problem."

They drove back toward Fort Lauderdale in silence. She lowered the visor, checked her face in the mirror. There was a faint bruise on the left side of her jaw, finger marks on her neck. Makeup would hide them.

"You know," he said, "we may have taken him out of commission for a while, but he won't give up. Way we left it, sooner or later he'll come looking for us."

"Let him," she said.

She got into New York the next day, tired and sore, her jaw aching. She'd slept fitfully on the train, her legs restless.

She carried her suitcase and shoulder bag through Penn Station, rode the escalator up into a bitter wind. A street-corner Santa rang his bell over a red plastic chimney. She dropped a five in, joined the line of people at the taxi stand.

Twenty minutes later, she was in her apartment, ears still stinging from the cold. She was exhausted but too wired to sleep. She left the bags in the living room, opened a bottle of wine. She filled a glass, carried it into the bedroom, and booted up the laptop.

A Google search on "Fort Lauderdale" and "robbery" brought her to the *South Florida Sun-Sentinel* Web site. The story was the third down on the Local News page: NEW JERSEY MAN KILLED IN BROWARD HOLDUP. The story was bare bones, five paragraphs, no quotes. A Louis Letteri of Belleville, New Jersey, had been shot to death in an armed robbery at the La Paloma hotel in Fort Lauderdale Beach. There was no mention of a card game. Police were seeking witnesses.

She sipped wine, ran another search on "Louis Letteri," came up with nothing.

When she went back into the living room to refill her glass, the black cat with the torn ear was at the window. It had come up the fire escape, was perched on the ledge, watching her.

It backed away when she neared the window. She undid the locks, pushed up the sash and storm window.

"You might as well come in," she said. "The damage is done."

The cat leaped from the sill to the floor, brushed against her legs. It moved around the room, evaluating its surroundings. She shut the window, locked it.

When she turned, the cat was lying on the futon, watching her warily.

You've got the right idea, she thought. Grab a warm place to sleep when you can, but don't trust anyone too much.

She let the cat have the futon, turned the radio on, the volume low, Beethoven's *Moonlight Sonata* coming soft from the speakers.

She went into the bedroom, cracked a Lunesta in half, washed it down with wine. She pulled off her boots, lay on the comforter fully clothed. She could still feel the rocking of the train, but the pain in her jaw was fading.

She closed her eyes, let the wine and music take her, the miles and anxiety of the past week slipping away. In seconds, she was asleep.

FOURTEEN

The girl couldn't have been more than eighteen. Eddie watched her from the bed as she dressed, pissed that Tino's man had sent over someone so young. She was Puerto Rican, dark and skinny, but with flesh where it mattered. They hadn't talked much. He'd done her twice before he'd asked her name.

Now she was brushing her hair in the motel room mirror, ignoring him. She wore a black blouse, tight jeans, and heels.

"Maria," he said.

She didn't turn.

"That's your name, right?"

"Marisol." She kept brushing.

He pushed the sheets away, got up, walked naked to the desk. Tino had sent a bottle of Glenlivet as well. Eddie dropped ice cubes into a motel glass, poured an inch of Scotch. The bottle was still half full.

"You have something for me?" she said.

"Didn't Tino take care of you?"

"I don't know any Tino. Is Esteban gave me the address."

"You don't know any Tino. But you know Nicky, right? Tino's son?"

"*Sí.* I know Nicholas."

He sipped Scotch. "You fuck him?"

She pulled on a puffy red jacket.

"It's not nice to talk that way," she said. "Nicholas has been very good to me."

"How old are you?"

"Twenty-two."

"Bullshit."

She buttoned the jacket, stood there waiting.

He put the glass on the nightstand, next to the phone Nicky had given him. He got his wallet from his coat.

"How much?" he said.

"Two hundred."

He counted out twenties, looked at her. She was chewing gum. He found himself stirring again. He folded the bills, dropped them beside the glass.

"Come here."

"Anything now is extra."

"Take off that coat."

She did, hung it on a chair. With her back to him, she started to undress. He thought about going over there, hitting her hard in the face, knocking the attitude out of her, then doing her right there on the carpet.

When she got the jeans off, he saw the finger marks he'd left on her hips and thighs, tiny bruised spots.

"Leave the thong on," he said. "Come over here."

He thought about calling Terry, inviting him over to tear off a piece while she was here, wondered if he'd do it.

She stood in front of him.

"Don't fucking look at me like that," he said. "Get on your knees."

"That's fifty more." She took the gum out.

"You know something? Esteban won't protect you. Neither will Nicky. They don't give a shit about you. They gave you to me."

"Don't say that."

"I could do anything I wanted to you. I could kill you right here and they wouldn't care. They'd help me get rid of your body." The bored look was gone now, the first trace of fear in her eyes.

"That's not true," she said.

He held his hands out, turned them over to show her the veins, the knobbed knuckles.

"See these?" he said. "I could beat you bloody with these. Break your ribs, your arms. Your jaw. Do whatever I wanted."

She looked back at the door.

"You'd never make it," he said.

The phone on the nightstand began to ring.

Terry steered the El Camino into the supermarket lot. Only the black SUV back here now. It was almost midnight. After he'd spoken with Nicky, Eddie had sent the whore away with her money, called Terry.

Terry parked, killed the lights. Eddie took the Star from the small of his back, eased the slide back to check there was a round in the chamber. He slipped the gun in a coat pocket.

"You bringing that in?" Terry said.

"You never know. If it sounds like things are going bad, haul ass out of here."

"What do you mean?"

"Just what I said." He got out.

When he reached the rear door, Vincent Rio opened it from inside. The motion sensor light stayed off.

"Hey," Rio said.

Eddie went down the cinder-block hall to the office. Tino was in there alone, a cup of takeout coffee in his hand. He stood as Eddie came in.

"Thanks for coming so quick," he said.

Eddie nodded. Rio moved in behind him at the door.

"Have a seat," Tino said. Eddie dragged a folding chair close, sat.

"I'll be out back," Rio said. Tino shut the door behind him.

"Where's Nicky?" Eddie said.

"I didn't want Nick here. Not for this."

Eddie rested his hands on his thighs. The gun was a weight in his coat.

"A terrible thing has happened," Tino said. He sat, put the cup on the desk. "You heard about my son-in-law?"

Eddie shook his head. "Do I know him?"

"You met him, maybe. One time or another. Lou Letteri, Ginny's husband."

Eddie shrugged.

"I'm getting too old for this," Tino said. "I thought I was used to anything, there was nothing I hadn't seen, couldn't deal with. But this . . ."

"What happened?"

"Lou's been down in Florida last few months. He and Ginny weren't getting along, husband and wife stuff, you know? Nothing serious, except he liked to gamble, on anything, horses, football, cards, whatever. Would drop a hundred grand in Vegas on a weekend without blinking."

"Okay," Eddie said.

"So he owes money all over the place, you know? Owes me money, too, but I'm his father-in-law, what am I supposed to do? Tell my daughter her husband's a degenerate gambler, he's pissing away their kids' college fund? They've got two daughters, Lisa and Linda, ten and six, beautiful little girls." He tapped his chest. "I love them like you wouldn't believe."

Eddie looked at the TV screen. Rio stood by the back door, smoking a cigarette. He looked up into the camera lens, as if he could see them inside. Eddie looked back at Tino.

"So he's down there in Florida, doing some things for me, but mainly staying out of trouble, taking it easy. A time-out for him and Ginny, you know? And he gets involved in this weekly card game down there, high rollers. He shouldn't even be in it, God knows where he got the money, but he can't stay away. So night before last, he's playing, some hotel in Fort Lauderdale, and the game gets knocked over. Pros."

"What makes you say that?"

"Report I got. Or almost pros, I should say. Lou's problem,

his whole life, he can't keep his mouth shut. The heisters are in there, waving their guns around—one's got a rifle—and he starts giving them shit. One of them gets itchy. Boom. Right there at the table."

"They shot him?"

Tino nodded.

"Dead?"

"We're flying his body back up here this week. My daughter's a wreck. The girls . . . what can you tell them?"

"Sounds like he was in the wrong place, wrong time."

"Exactly. But it doesn't make it easier, for anyone."

"They get away?"

Tino nodded.

"Anyone else hurt?"

"Just Lou. They took off right after that. Got all the money, though. A half million, I'm hearing."

"That's a heavy card game. And they knew when to hit it."

"Like I said, pros. They all wore masks, got out of there quick. The other players, too. Most of them were gone before the cops showed up."

"What do the police say?"

"Not much so far. But I have friends down there."

"And?"

"The crew that did it was from out of town," Tino said. "I got a name. The one that ran it, put it together. Same one that pulled the trigger."

"Where's he from?"

"Up here. Staten Island."

"He connected?"

"Not in any way that matters."

"Why'd you call me?"

"Who else can I trust?"

Eddie sat back. "Got out just in time, didn't I? What about Nicky? You'd think he'd want in on this, family and all."

"Nick's no good for this. Like I said, this guy was a pro. Nick's a good kid, but . . ."

"You don't want him involved in something that could go bad."

"He's my son. Is that wrong?"

"I guess not. What's in it?"

"Thirty. But it needs to be soon. There needs to be a message."

"Forty. I've got a partner."

"That kid?"

Eddie nodded.

"Do it for thirty," Tino said, "and keep whatever you find on him. There's got to be a chunk left from that game."

"You're bargaining."

"So?"

"I thought this was about family."

"It is."

"Forty. I just got out. I need to get back on my feet. I'll take twenty up front. The rest when it's done."

Tino raised his hands, let them fall. "Forty. But like I said, it needs to be quick. The faster, the better. Just find him and do it."

"What about the rest of his crew?"

"Don't worry about them. They're all over the country by now anyway. Besides, those people have no loyalty to each other. They won't care what happens to him. No, just the one. The one that pulled the trigger. The one that planned it."

"What's the name?"

"Victor Stimmer. You know him?"

Eddie shook his head.

"Word is he's back up here already," Tino said.

"Why?"

"Maybe he's got noplace else to go."

"You have an address?"

"He owns an electronics store on Amboy Road. Lives nearby. I've got a photo of him, too. Bald guy, blue eyes, hard to miss. He gets wind someone's looking for him, though, he'll take off. Another reason it needs to be quick."

"When do I get the twenty?"

"Tomorrow morning, if you want. Nick will bring it where you're staying. The picture, too."

"Okay." He stood.

"You're like a son to me," Tino said, "and I want you to know that. There was no one else I could go to with this. No one else I could trust."

Eddie nodded, opened the door.

"You've got nothing to worry about," he said. "I'll handle it."

Vincent Rio was still at the rear door. Eddie nodded at him, went out to the El Camino. As they pulled out of the lot, Terry said, "How'd it go?"

Eddie rolled down his window, felt the cold air on his face. "About as expected. I guess I never learn."

"Learn what?"

"Never mind."

"What did he want? He have something for us?"

"Yeah."

"What is it?"

"What I thought," Eddie said. "Nigger work."

FIFTEEN

She was coming out of the D'Agostino's on 110th, plastic grocery bags dangling from both hands, when her cell began to buzz. She backed into a gated doorway, out of the flow of people on the sidewalk, juggled the bags to get the phone out. Hector. It buzzed again, then went quiet.

When she got home, the cat was curled on the futon. It leaped off as she came in, slunk into the kitchen, watching her over its shoulder. She fed it every day, but it still wouldn't let her touch it.

She left the bags on the living room floor, called Hector back. He picked up on the second ring.

"*Hola,*" she said. "I owe you something, I know. I have it."

"Not why I called. Can we meet?"

"What's up?"

"Better in person."

"This about work? If so, I'm not interested."

"Old work, not new."

"What's that mean?"

"I'm midtown right now, I can be up your way in about twenty."

She didn't like that, but there was no use asking more over the phone.

"Call me when you get up here," she said. "I'll tell you where I'll be."

At the Starbucks on 114th, she got a high table by the window, had a clear view up and down Broadway. The rest of the tables were occupied by students, most reading or tapping on laptops. She set the paper Garden of Eden bag at her feet, blew steam from her tea.

She saw him from a block away. He crossed Broadway against the light, came in. She cocked her head at the counter. He nodded and joined the line.

When he carried his cup to the table, she said, "Take a seat. Just relax for a couple minutes. Drink your coffee."

He nodded, sat across from her, popped the lid from his cup. He blew on it, sipped.

"Cold out there," he said. "What happened to your jaw?"

"Walked into something. No big deal."

"That happen down there?"

She drank tea, didn't answer. He put his cup down, unzipped his flight jacket. He held it open, then raised his sweatshirt for a moment to show her his bare chest and stomach, pulled it down again.

She looked around to see if anyone else had noticed. "That wasn't really necessary. But if you enjoy it . . ."

He shrugged. "Can't be too careful, right?"

"So, old work."

"I don't have a lot of information yet. Just wanted to share what I know."

"Share."

"The guy that got dealt out of the game down south . . . he was somebody."

"What's that mean?"

"Connected. He was from up here, across the river."

"Jersey?"

He nodded, sipped coffee. "One of my brother's old partners moves in those circles sometimes. Word was getting around."

"And?"

"It checks out."

"How connected?"

"Close. Family."

"Nothing like that in the news stories. I've been checking every day."

"It's true, though."

She sat back, looked out the window, watched steam rise from manhole covers. She felt the first stirrings of an upset stomach, the tea not sitting well.

"I thought this couldn't possibly be more fucked up than it already was," she said. "I guess I was wrong."

"I don't know what happened with our friend down there. He's been a solid guy up to now. And it sounded good."

"It *was* good. Until it wasn't."

"There's another thing, too. I hear he's back. Up here."

"Already? Then he's stupider than I thought. He looking for me?"

"I don't know."

"You need to be careful, too," she said. "He knows you."

"If he's looking, I'll hear about it. If it comes to that, I'll handle him."

"This just keeps getting better, doesn't it?"

She looked out at the traffic. If Stimmer was back, he had to still be in bad shape from the beating he'd taken. In no shape to be on the hunt.

"We have to get a message to our other friend," she said. "With the tattoos."

"My thought, too. I'll call his man." Chance's contact was a retired bank robber in Missouri named Sladden.

"If there's fallout on this from across the river," she said, "it's on one person."

"I know."

"He put us all in danger down there, then tried to take us off. He did what he did. He's on his own."

"Understood."

She edged the bag closer to him under the table.

"That's for you. A little better than last time. Twenty and change. That should take care of those Communion clothes."

"*Gracias.*"

"That's dirty. Raw. Just so you know."

"Understood."

She finished her tea. The ache in her stomach was a dull burning now. She looked at people hurrying along the sidewalk. A different world.

"Sorry about all this," he said.

"What's done is done. There's no going back."

"No," he said. "There never is."

Back in the apartment, she got the maroon suitcase from the closet, opened it on the bed. It was always packed, ready to go. Two weeks' worth of clothes in it, and thirty thousand in cash—all hundred-dollar bills—sewn into the lining, slight bulges through the material. Tomorrow she'd get the .38 from the bank, keep it in the apartment. If Stimmer came looking for her, she would have to be ready.

She switched out some of the clothes, packed everything neatly again, then closed the suitcase. She looked at the laptop on the desk. She'd loaded Maddie's new photos onto it, would want to bring it with her if she had to leave. She'd used one of the pictures as a screensaver, then taken it down after a day. It hurt too much to look at it.

She heard a noise, turned to see the cat watching her from the doorway.

"What are you looking at?"

She'd gotten used to having it around. It made the apartment seem less empty. She hadn't named it, though, wouldn't. The next time she left town, she'd put it back out on the fire escape, let it fend for itself again.

The cat leaped onto the desk in one fluid movement, crouched there, eyeing her.

"What's your problem? You think you were just going to move in here, live happily ever after? Who gets that?"

She latched the suitcase, put it back in the closet. It felt good to have it here, ready.

It would feel better when she had the gun.

SIXTEEN

"He's not there," Eddie said, "and he's not coming back either."

It was their second night watching the house. The street was lined with trees, so they were able to park in shadow. The photo Nicky had given them was on the dashboard. It was a mug shot, a couple years old, but good enough that Eddie would recognize the man if he saw him.

"Left the country if he's smart," Terry said.

"Tino said he was back here."

"I don't know. Doesn't make sense."

"No, it doesn't," Eddie said. "Go creep the place, see what you turn up."

Terry didn't answer.

"You can still handle that, right?"

"Not anymore, Eddie. Like I said, I haven't done that in years."

"I'm sure you still got the touch. You have tools?"

"Maybe a couple."

"Good enough. Let's go get them."

Eddie waited in the El Camino, caught glimpses of light moving around in the second-floor windows. Terry up there with a penlight.

Fifteen minutes later, a shadow detached itself from the trees out front, started down the street. Terry walking fast.

He got behind the wheel, his face pale. There was sweat on his forehead despite the cold. He took a chamois bag from under his coat and slid it beneath the seat.

"What's the word?" Eddie said.

Terry tugged at his gloves, had trouble getting them off.

"Relax," Eddie said. "You're clear. What did you find?"

"Not much. Dust in there, no one's been home for a while. It was wired, though. I had to bypass the alarm system on a back window."

"See, I told you. You never forget."

Terry took a business card from his coat pocket, handed it over. It read ALLIED ELECTRONICS, a Staten Island address and phone number beneath it. "A whole box of these in the kitchen."

"Find any cash?"

"Nothing. And no sign of a safe anywhere."

"You holding out on me?"

"Eddie, I would never do that."

"I know." He put the card away. "Good job."

Terry started the engine. They made their way back to Richmond Parkway, could see the lights of the Outerbridge in the distance. Terry got a cigarette from his pack, dropped it, had to bend to pick it up from the floor mat.

"Got the adrenaline going again, huh?" Eddie said. "Feels good, doesn't it?"

Terry punched in the dashboard lighter. When it popped, he lit the cigarette. Eddie let him.

"We'll check out the store tomorrow," he said. "See if he shows up. Mornings right before they open, at night when they close. Doubt he'd show his face there during the day, people looking for him."

They reached the bridge, the steel roadway humming under them, the lights of Jersey ahead.

"I'm worried about Ange," Terry said. "I don't like leaving her alone at night like this."

"Maybe you should call your friend Cody, have him stop by."

Terry was silent.

"She's got a phone," Eddie said. "She has a problem, she can call someone. She'll be fine. Crack that window a little, let that shit out."

Terry rolled down the window. Wind sucked out the smoke.

"Anyway," Eddie said, "sooner we find this guy, the better."

"What happens then?"

"What do you think?"

Allied Electronics anchored a strip mall on Amboy Road, in sight of Raritan Bay. They'd parked behind it, in the lot of a liquor store across the street. They had a view of the alley behind the mall, the service doors and loading docks. That morning they'd watched as employees parked, went in to open the stores.

Now it was 10:00 P.M. and they were drinking McDonald's coffee, watching the alley. They had come back here at nine and parked in the same spot, the liquor store closed for the night.

Terry had smoked a half-dozen cigarettes since they'd gotten there, the window half open. Now his right foot was tapping steadily on the floorboard.

"Knock that shit off," Eddie said.

Terry fumbled with his cigarette pack.

"Give it a break," Eddie said.

Terry put the pack away. "I was wondering. Those things you were saying the other night. About Tino."

"What about them?"

"If the guy pisses you off so much, why are we helping him out?"

"I need him. For now. Need his cash, his connections. What burns me is he still acts like he runs the show, like things are the way they used to be. You see that shithole he was hanging out in? What does that tell you?"

"But he's still the man. I mean, in North Jersey at least, right?"

"He may think he is, but he's pushing seventy, just beat one case, already indicted on another. Most of his money goes to lawyers. And his kid's useless. I don't know what he has in mind for him, but whatever it is, he's not up to it."

"Still, I wouldn't want to fuck with either of them."

"What makes you think I am?"

"I'm just saying."

"Their days are over," Eddie said. "Him and all those guys. If he's lucky, he'll die before that case ever goes to trial. He's done. He just won't accept it."

They watched people get into cars, drive away. By eleven, there was only one car in the lot, a Corvette parked directly behind the electronics store.

"Someone's staying late," Eddie said.

Headlights turned down the alley, lighting up Dumpsters and wooden pallets.

"Heads up," Eddie said.

It was a black BMW with tinted windows. It pulled up alongside the Corvette, doused its lights. Almost on cue, the store's rear door opened. A man stood there, outlined against the light.

Eddie put the half-full coffee cup on the floor, took Stimmer's photo from the dashboard. The BMW's lights went out.

"Think that's him?" Terry said.

"Quiet."

The driver got out, reached back in, and drew out a pair of crutches.

He hipped the door shut, used the crutches to limp up the steps. The man held the door for him. In the light, Eddie could see the driver's shaven head, wide shoulders. They went inside, the door closing behind them.

"That's him," Eddie said.

"What do we do?"

"We wait."

Ten minutes later, the door opened again, and Stimmer came out. He made his way down the steps, a small canvas bag tucked under his arm. Eddie could see him grimace with every step.

"Guy's fucked up," Terry said.

Stimmer got the driver's side door of the BMW open, tossed the bag in, fumbled with the crutches. He put them in the backseat, slid behind the wheel.

"He's skimming the till," Eddie said. "Getting them to put money aside for him. Or he keeps some in there regular, a safe maybe."

The BMW's lights went on. It backed out of the space.

"Get on him," Eddie said.

He led them back to Jersey. They crossed the Outerbridge again, drove for twenty minutes before the BMW turned onto Route 22 West, down into Middlesex County. They followed a safe distance behind, neither of them talking.

The BMW slowed. They were in Plainfield now, old two-story houses hard against the side of the highway. Peeling paint, no front yards. The BMW turned without signaling, pulled into a narrow driveway and around the back of a house.

"Take this next right," Eddie said. "Then pull over."

Terry made the turn, steered the El Camino to the curb, killed the engine and lights. They could see the BMW's headlights in a backyard two houses down.

"Come on," Eddie said.

They got out of the El Camino and crossed into the first yard, a concrete patio with clotheslines strung across it. They ducked beneath, came to a chest-high wooden fence. In the next yard, the BMW's headlights lit up a garage, wood stairs leading up the side, the windows dark.

Stimmer got out of the BMW, balancing on the crutches, and fought the garage door up and open. Then he got back in the BMW, drove it inside. The headlights went out.

Eddie took thin leather gloves from a coat pocket, pulled them on.

"Maybe I should wait here, keep an eye out," Terry said.

"No. You come with me." He put his hands on top of the fence, vaulted it, dropped down quietly on the other side, staying in the shadows.

Stimmer crutch-walked out of the garage, the canvas bag under his arm again, and got the door closed. He stopped to rest, wiped sweat from his face, then started up the stairs.

Eddie heard Terry come over the fence behind him. Stimmer reached the door of the garage apartment, got keys out. He almost dropped the bag, but trapped it between his elbow and side, while he unlocked the door. Eddie crossed the yard to the stairs, went up without sound.

When Stimmer opened the door, Eddie came up behind, shoved him hard. Stimmer stumbled into the room beyond, the crutches tangling, and went down on his side. Eddie drew the Star, kicked the crutches away, pointed the gun at the dark doorway of the next room. No movement or sound.

Stimmer was wheezing, pulling at the zipper of his jacket. Eddie crouched over him, put the muzzle of the Star against his temple. Terry came up the stairs.

"Come on in," Eddie said. "Close the door."

SEVENTEEN

Stimmer's gun was a black Ruger automatic, 9 mm. Eddie tossed it on the couch, searched him with his free hand. In Stimmer's right pants pocket was a straight razor with a bone handle. Eddie put it beside the gun.

"Watch him," he said to Terry.

He walked through the apartment. Living room, bedroom, eat-in kitchen, and bathroom. A few clothes in a bedroom bureau, nothing in the closet but an empty suitcase. He went back into the living room, turned on a table lamp.

Stimmer had rolled into a sitting position. Eddie could see the fading bruises on his face, a purple spot on the side of his jaw.

Eddie picked up the canvas bag, tossed it to Terry. "Check that out." Stimmer was watching them.

"Wallet," Eddie said.

Stimmer's eyes were watery with pain, but no fear. He

reached behind, drew out a thick wallet, tossed it at Eddie's feet. Eddie picked it up, sat on the couch.

"What do you want?" Stimmer said.

Eddie ignored him, put the Star away, looked though the wallet. Two hundred in cash, credit cards, and a driver's license. He took the cash out, tossed the wallet back at him.

"You know who I am?" Eddie said.

Stimmer shook his head.

"Sometimes they call me Eddie the Saint. That mean anything to you?"

"Should it?"

"Who fucked you up?"

Stimmer looked away.

"Ten thousand," Terry said. He put the money back in the bag.

To Stimmer, Eddie said, "Any more of that around here?"

"That's it."

Eddie turned to Terry. "Have a look around."

Terry set the money bag on the couch, left the room.

Eddie picked up the Ruger, then went to the front door and locked it.

"Fucking Tino," Stimmer said.

Eddie turned to him. "What?"

"Nothing."

They heard noises from the bedroom. Terry came back out holding banded stacks of cash.

"Loose floorboards in the closet," he said. "Maybe twenty thousand all together."

Eddie looked at Stimmer. "Lying bastard."

Stimmer raised himself to a sitting position. He was still breathing heavily.

"I think you and I need to have a conversation," Eddie said. "Fill me in on some things, and you'll get out of this all right."

"Yeah? Fill this in: Go fuck yourself."

"That money in the floor, that from Fort Lauderdale?"

"Never been there."

"Twenty grand in there, and ten grand from the store tonight. You planning to make a run for it?"

"Why would I do that?"

"You're a hard guy," Eddie said. "I get it. An OG. But I am, too, so where's that leave us?"

"It leaves me fucking your mother where she breathes."

"Okay. Another approach." He set the Ruger on the arm of the couch, picked up the razor. To Terry, he said, "Go find me some duct tape or something, a dish towel. Anything I can use as a gag." He opened the blade.

"Gag on this," Stimmer said and touched his crotch.

"You got balls, I'll give you that. Maybe that's where we should start."

"I ain't saying shit to you about anything. If you came here to do me, you piece of shit, then do it."

"Who says I came here to do you? All I want is the cash."

"You got it already. All I have."

Eddie shook his head. "Three of you, five hundred grand on the table? No, you've got more than that somewhere."

"I don't know what you're talking about."

"I look stupid to you, OG? That the way this conversation is going to go?"

"Do what you gotta do."

"I will," Eddie said. "But when this shit gets bad, remember it was your fault."

Terry came back in with a white T-shirt. "All I could find."

"That'll do." Eddie stood, razor in hand. "Wind it tight, tie it over his mouth."

Terry hesitated.

"Do it."

"Wait," Stimmer said. "Just wait a minute."

"Why?"

Stimmer looked at Terry, then back to Eddie. "You're not going to let me walk out of here. I know that."

"Don't be so sure. I want the money, that's all. I don't care about your sad, beaten-up ass."

"You got the money. All I have."

Eddie closed the razor, dropped it in a pocket. "How do you know Tino?"

"Tino who?"

"Tino who gave me this, told me where you lived." He took the picture out, showed it to him.

"That motherfucker," Stimmer said.

"He is that. How do you know him?"

"I got nothing to say about that."

Eddie picked up the Ruger, racked the slide. The chambered shell ejected as another loaded, the hammer locking back. He set the gun back down.

"So, if that's all you've got," Eddie said, "where's the rest of the money?"

Stimmer took a breath. "I don't have it. That bitch and her partner do."

"Who's that?"

"I thought you knew all about it."

"I'm asking you."

"Cell phone."

"Go ahead."

Stimmer reached into a jacket pocket, drew out a phone. He put it on the floor, slid it across to Eddie's feet.

"Why do I want that?" Eddie said.

"Let's understand each other. You want that money, from Fort Lauderdale. I don't have it, but I can lead you to the people who do."

"And who would that be?"

"One of them is named Bobby Chance. You heard of him?"

"No."

"He works out of the Midwest mostly. The other one's a woman. Named Crissa Stone."

"Bullshit."

"Ask around. She used to run with a pro named Wayne Boudreaux, they worked together. Now he's inside and she's on her own. She and Chance fucked me over, took the whole haul."

"They the ones that put the beating on you?"

"Yeah. Left me down there with a broken kneecap and three cracked ribs. And they took every dime."

"How much was that?"

"My third was supposed to be a hundred and forty K. You can do the math yourself. They kept it all."

"So you've got a score to settle with them?"

"Wouldn't you?"

"What about Letteri, the one who got shot?"

"What about him?"

"You pulled the trigger, you tell me."

"Whoever told you that is a fucking liar. Chance fired that shot. They tried to lay that on me afterward, too."

Eddie sat back down. After a moment, he said, "Something doesn't make sense."

"You're right, there was close to half a mil in that game. And the two of them took it all and framed me up for the shooting. So, yeah, I got a score to settle."

"So, maybe we can help you with that. Where are they now?"

"In the wind, but they couldn't have gotten far. Like I said, Chance is in the Midwest these days, but Stone used to be based up here, New York maybe."

"How'd you get in touch with them?"

"I didn't. They have contacts they work through. I put word out I was looking to put a crew together. They were available."

"How'd you reach the contacts?"

Stimmer nodded at the phone. "It's all in there. I've met Stone's guy. His name's Hector Suarez. He's up here, Jersey City. Chance's guy is named Sladden, out of Missouri. Take a look for yourself. Their numbers are both in there."

"Tell me more," Eddie said. "Everything you know about them."

Stimmer talked for the next five minutes. Eddie scratched his chin, occasionally looking over to where Terry stood.

When Stimmer was done, Eddie said, "Okay, I believe you. But it doesn't look like you're in much shape to go looking for anyone."

"I'm not. Not yet, at least. But I can help you."

"And what are you expecting out of this?"

"I'm not expecting anything. I just want to settle it. You give me whatever you think is fair. Or nothing at all, that's fine with me, too."

"It's the principle of the thing," Eddie said.

"Something like that."

"You say you've got Suarez's number in there?"

"Yes."

"Show me."

"Why?"

"Because I need to know if you're bullshitting us or not."

Stimmer picked up the phone, punched keys. He held up the illuminated screen so Eddie could see it.

"Right there," he said. "HS." Eddie nodded.

"He's a family man," Stimmer said. He closed the phone, set it back on the floor. "Wife and kids. But he's a hard case, or at least tries to act like it."

"Stand up," Eddie said.

Stimmer pulled his crutches closer, got them under him.

"You need a hand?" Eddie said.

"No, I'm good." He rose slowly, looked at Terry. "You need to leave me some of that money. It's all I've got."

"Don't push it," Eddie said. "So where do we start?"

"Suarez. We get him to tell us where Stone is, she leads us to Chance. They both lead us to the money. There hasn't been much time, they've probably still got most of it. They'll be sitting on it, waiting for the heat to blow over."

"That would be the smart thing," Eddie said.

"Oh, they're smart, all right."

"Could be tough finding them, though."

"I've worked with both of them before. I know them, I know people they know. I can find them. I just need help."

"Okay."

"When we find that Stone bitch, though, I want to handle it myself."

"I don't blame you," Eddie said. He sat thinking for a moment, then stood.

"Listen up," he said. "Here's the deal. You help us find Suarez. He takes us to Stone. Whatever we get from her, my partner and I"—he looked at Terry—"split three-quarters of it. You get what's left. That's if we find anything."

Stimmer nodded, rested his weight on the crutches. "That'll work," he said. "And don't worry, we'll find them all right."

"I'm not worried," Eddie said. He lifted the Ruger and shot him through the forehead.

EIGHTEEN

She felt calmer out of the city. It was a two-and-a-half-hour drive to Litchfield, another twenty minutes on a rural road north of town. It was colder up here, snow still on the ground, the trees bare.

The house was set back from the road, thick woods on three sides, the trees dark and naked. Windblown snow covered half the FOR SALE sign on a post in the yard.

She steered the rented Saturn up the driveway, parked in front of the single-car garage on the edge of the woods. The backyard was an unmarred sheet of white.

The first time she'd seen the house, she'd fallen in love with it. It was a two-story colonial, built in the early 1900s, simple in design and detail, but with the look of permanence. It had been freshly painted since she'd last been here, white with green trim. Sunlight flashed off the big windows of the enclosed back porch.

Against the garage wall was a pile of snow-topped firewood. She thought of the big fireplace in the living room, the brick hearth. Imagined building a fire while snow fell outside. This is the house I've always wanted, she thought. The house I've earned.

She got out her cell, called the Realtor in Litchfield. When the woman answered, all Crissa said was "I'm here."

The Realtor's name was Jackie. She was in her forties, with long blond hair and a hippieish quality despite her business suit.

"I know you've already been through here once," she said as she unlocked the front door, "but I'm sure the Hammersteins won't mind your coming back. Like we say in the business, they're motivated."

She led Crissa into the big front room. The hardwood floor was dusty, the couch and chairs covered with sheets. Everything looked exactly as it had the first time she'd been here, three months ago.

"When was the last time someone lived here?" Crissa said.

"Six months maybe? The Hammersteins are in the Caymans most of the time now. He has business there. But they have someone come by every once in a while. I stop by now and then, too. They leave the power on."

"Is there an alarm?"

"No. We don't have much crime up here. You could leave your doors unlocked and not have to worry about anything."

"I doubt that," Crissa said.

"Well, you're from the city. Things are different down there."

They walked through the dining room and into the kitchen.

"Still," Crissa said. "Seems like they're taking a chance, leaving the house empty so long."

"Up here, it's like a small town. Everyone knows everyone. Unless you don't want them to, of course. I mean, it's very private, too."

They went out onto the porch. Light poured through the tall windows, warming the trapped air. She had a vision of the cat with the torn ear curled on the sill, sleeping in the sun. This would be a good room, she thought. A room to sit in when you grew old.

"It's an old house, but charming," Jackie said. "It just needs a little work here and there."

"That's okay. I'm handy." She looked out into the snowy expanse of yard, the trees beyond. "What about the neighbors?"

"The Coopers are down the road a ways. If you look to the left there, you can almost see their house through the trees. He's an architect, she's a party planner. They have a condo in Manhattan, so they're mainly up here in the summer. Sometimes weekends during the fall, too. The leaves around here then are unbelievable."

"What about the other side?"

"That's very sad."

"Why?"

"Mr. Dubro, who owns it with his wife, worked for a big insurance company in the city. There were some shenanigans with mortgages or something, I don't know what exactly. The company went under, and he ended up in some sort of trouble. They tried to sell the house, but the way the market's been . . ."

"It could have been worse," Crissa said. "He could have gone to prison, lost the house altogether."

"I guess that's true."

"Kids in the neighborhood?"

"No, not nearby at least. You're probably glad to hear that."

"No. It would be nice if there were. How are the schools?"

"Most of the children bus into the next county. The middle school there always makes the list of the state's best. Do you want to take another look upstairs?"

Crissa nodded, and they went up to the second floor. Two bedrooms here, a bathroom with new tiling and an old clawfoot tub. She went into the rear bedroom, Jackie following. The room smelled of dust and mothballs. The bed was stripped, the other furniture covered with sheets.

At the window, Crissa looked down on the gleaming white yard. She had a clear view of the driveway, the garage, and the woods beyond. A dead wasp lay on the sill.

"Great exposure in here, as you can see," Jackie said, "and quite a view."

A bird landed on the woodpile, pecked at the snow, flew away.

It would be a different world up here, Crissa thought. Far from the city. A house to call her own, with land, not just a cramped apartment with three rooms, noise in the street all night. A new life, if she could afford it. A place to come home to.

"So what's the holdup?" she said.

"Holdup?"

"On the offer I made. You said they were motivated."

"I'm not sure. I guess they're having some issues deciding. There are several offers on the table."

"With sixty percent down? Two hundred and fifty thousand cash?"

"I'm sure they're taking that into consideration."

"My lawyer says they want to know more about my background."

"That could be, I don't—"

"Is it because I'm a single woman? They're wondering where the money's coming from?"

"I really can't speak for them."

"I'm not going higher, if that's what this is about."

You can't afford to anyway, she thought. Thinking about Wayne then, in his jailhouse khakis. Wondering if, when it came down to it, she would have to choose.

"I'll talk with them again," Jackie said. "They're going to call me this week from Grand Cayman."

"I think we've got the same goal. You want to close the deal, earn your commission."

"Of course, but—"

"So maybe a time frame will help them decide. Say a month from today. We get the inspectors in, and, if there's nothing major, I cut the Hammersteins a cashier's check for the down payment, and we get the lawyers going on the closing." Trying to be casual, not have it sound like a threat.

"I'll talk to them."

"After that date, who knows," Crissa said. "I'm looking at some other places, too, in Plymouth and Torrington." Lying.

"I'll do my best."

"I know you will. Thank you." She extended her hand, and Jackie looked at it for a moment, then took it.

"Make it clear to them," Crissa said. "One month. Or I walk."

"I'll let them know."

"And let them know one other thing."

"What's that?"

"I don't bluff."

Later, she drove into Litchfield, parked on Bantam Road, and walked along the row of antique shops. Christmas music was playing everywhere. She stopped to watch an electric train display in a toy store window.

It had started to snow again, the sky a hard gray. She decided then not to drive back to the city. There was a motel just outside of town she'd stayed in once before, a restaurant across the street. She'd have dinner and a couple of drinks, get a good night's rest, head back tomorrow. Or maybe stay another day, drive around a little, get more of a feel for the town.

She thought about Stimmer, back in the city, maybe looking for her and Chance. The thought of it made her angry. But if he surfaced, Hector would hear about it, let her know. She'd worry about it when the time came.

There was no hurry to get back. Up here, it felt right somehow, as if things were in balance. It felt like the future. It felt like home.

The second time he came over, Crissa realized the man in the flannel shirt was hitting on her.

She was sitting at the bar with a glass of red wine, looking up at the TV. It was a game show she'd never seen before, lanky models displaying metal cases on pedestals. The sound was turned down. Soft music leaked through from the adjoining restaurant.

She'd left the Saturn at the motel, walked over. She'd had a meal and a glass of wine in the restaurant, decided to do the rest of her drinking at the bar. It was an old building, weathered oak paneling, colonial prints on the wall. A gas fire flickered in a flagstone hearth, warming the room. Light snow blew against the windows.

The man in the flannel shirt came up behind her, empty glass in hand. She watched his approach in the bar mirror. He stood close to her, though there was only one other person at the bar. He set his glass down, signaled the bartender.

She was on her third glass of wine and feeling relaxed for the first time in weeks. She'd left her cell in the motel room, felt freed by its absence.

"Hi. My name's Travis."

She turned to him, ready to cut him off, shut him down. Late twenties, Levi's and green flannel, boots. Dark hair and brown eyes, a hint of five o'clock shadow. His cologne was faint and musky.

"Sorry if I'm interrupting," he said. "I thought I'd introduce myself. Since we're both alone."

She looked over at the table where he'd been sitting, the leather jacket hung on the chair, then back at him.

"Maybe that's a choice I made," she said.

"Aha," he said. "Sorry about that."

The bartender set his drink down. He took it and started to the table.

"Hold on," she said. He turned.

"I'm sorry," she said. "That was rude of me."

"No, I totally understand. I was out of line. I'll leave you alone."

"Come sit down."

He came back, slid onto the seat to her right. She put out her hand. "Roberta Summersfield. My friends call me Bobbi."

"Travis Unger." He shook her hand.

"Like Felix?"

"My curse in life."

"I apologize, Travis. I'm a little tired, that's all."

"I wasn't sure if I should come over. You look like you've got things on your mind."

"You have no idea."

When the bartender came back, she nodded. He filled her glass, took money. She was feeling the wine, the heat in the room, a pleasant light-headedness.

"I was being a little forward, I guess," he said. "Coming up on you like that. But I figured, what the hell?"

They drank as they talked. He was a carpenter from Long Valley, New Jersey, in Litchfield building custom cabinets at a pair of houses in town. He'd been here almost two weeks, he told her, and was feeling homesick.

"Don't you have an assistant?" she said. "Someone helps you with the work, lets you take a break for a couple days?"

"I did, but things got so slow, I had to let him go. It's starting to pick up a little now, but it's still not enough to keep two people working."

"Sorry to hear that."

"You here on business?"

"Looking at some houses," she said. "Maybe buying."

"That's a brave move these days. What do you do?"

"Investments. Here and there. Some property."

"A speculator."

"Sometimes."

"You like to take risks."

She shook her head. "Not me."

She was starting to warm to him now, his manner easy and relaxed.

"You up here from the city?" he said.

"Just until tomorrow."

"Are you married? You don't have to answer that."

"No, not married."

"Engaged? Someone special?"

She gave that a moment. "Yes."

"That's good. You have a slight accent. I've been trying to place it. It's very faint, and it's not New York."

"No, it isn't," she said, wondering how much to give him.

"So you want me to guess?"

"Texas," she said, "but that was a long time ago."

She sipped wine. It happened like this three or four times a year. The last had been in Tortola. She'd be away somewhere, under another name, and she'd meet someone this way, without trying. It would last a day or two at most, more often just a single night. It would take the edge off for a while, but without entanglements. She wasn't who they thought she was, so she owed them nothing.

"How about you?" she said. "Married?" She'd already seen the pale band on his finger where a ring had been.

"Divorced," he said.

"Sorry to hear that. How long?"

"Divorced? A year. Married, eight."

She thought about Wayne. Seven years now, three of those with him in lockup. Wondered what he would say if he saw her here now, talking to this man, smiling, drinking.

"Sorry," she said. "Drifting a little, I guess."

"I've probably overstayed my welcome. I guess we're both tired." He finished his drink.

She turned toward him. "Where are you staying while you're up here?"

"Across the street. I've been eating in here almost every night. It's starting to feel like home. How about you?"

"I'm there, too. There a liquor store around here?"

"Just a few blocks away," he said and smiled. "I've been there many times."

"When do they close?"

"Ten, maybe." He looked at his watch. "Still plenty of time."

"I'd like a little more of this," she said, touching the wineglass, "but not at these prices." Making the decision then, letting him know it.

"Sounds good to me," he said. "Let's go."

He had a big Ford 150 with a cap in back, EXCEL CARPENTRY and a phone number painted on the side. He drove carefully, not looking at her. Snow swirled in the headlights, the wipers clicking rhythmically. There were few cars on the road.

Outside the liquor store, she said, "Wait here," got out, and went inside. She bought a pint of rum and a liter of Coke for him, a bottle of Médoc for herself.

When they pulled into the motel lot, she said, "There's some plastic glasses in my room. Nothing fancy, but they'll do."

He took the bag from her, and they walked to her room in the snow. She closed the door against the wind, undid her scarf and unbuttoned her jacket. He set the bag on the table.

"Gotta hit the bathroom," he said.

"Go on."

Her cell was on the nightstand where she'd left it. She had three missed calls, all from Hector. No messages.

She hit RETURN CALL. He picked up on the second ring.

"Been trying to reach you all night," he said. "Can you talk?"

She looked at the closed bathroom door, heard the toilet flush, then the sound of running water.

"Yes. What's the problem?"

"It's about our friend. The bald guy with the blue eyes."

"What about him?"

"He's dead."

The bathroom door opened, and Travis came out, drying his hands on a towel. He looked at her, his smile fading. She lowered the phone.

"Travis," she said. "Go home."

NINETEEN

Hector suggested Hop Ling, but she was paranoid now, didn't want to meet anywhere they'd been before. They settled on a coffee shop on Church Street, near the World Trade Center PATH station.

She got there first, took a booth in the back, far from the windows. It was ten thirty in the morning, the breakfast crowd thinning. She was tired from the drive back, had left at first light. She was on her second cup of tea when he showed up and slid in across from her.

He ordered coffee from the waitress. When she walked away, Crissa said, "Tell it."

"I don't have all the details. Got a call from my cousin. She works with the state police, in the office."

"You never told me that."

"No reason to. She's a good source, I use her all the time. Back when Stimmer first got in touch, I asked her to run a check on him, see if there were any warrants, if he was involved in any open cases, listed as a CI, whatever."

"Was that smart?"

"She didn't know why. I'm just trying to keep you safe. If there'd been an issue, or something didn't seem right, I wouldn't have put you in touch with him."

The waitress brought his coffee, left. Crissa said, "What happened?"

"A crew working out in the Meadowlands, underground cables or something, found his car. He was in the trunk. One in the head. Hadn't been there long."

"It make the news?"

"Not yet. His wallet was in there with him, though. When my cousin saw the report, she called me. The car was under an abutment, out of sight. If that crew hadn't been there, it might not have been found for a while."

"Sounds like wiseguy bullshit."

"Maybe."

"Someone angry over Florida. Getting even."

"She'll call if she hears anything else."

"Question is, who else are they angry at? And what did he tell them beforehand?"

"That's why I called you last night. I figured you'd want to know right away. I called Chance's man, too. He's passing the message along."

"All that's been going on, he's probably halfway to Hawaii."

"Not a bad idea. Maybe you should think about the same. I sent Luisa and the girls to her mother's in Philly, just in case."

She looked around the room, scanning faces.

"I don't like this," she said. "Not knowing."

"What are you thinking?"

"Jimmy Falcone still around?"

"Which one, the father or the son?"

"The father. Jimmy Peaches."

"I think so. I haven't heard otherwise. Last I knew, he was in one of those assisted living places, down the Shore somewhere. Jimmy Junior's out in Marion, not coming home anytime soon. How do you know Jimmy Peaches?"

"Through Wayne. He pointed us to some work up here a few years back. I got to know him a little."

"He's old-school. Way before my time."

"Do me a favor and see what you can find out."

"I will. You know, there's a chance what happened to Stimmer has nothing to do with any of this. Could be an old beef he had. Could be something else entirely."

"That's right," she said. She finished the tea, got bills out for the check. "But do you really believe that?"

He didn't answer.

She was walking north on Broadway, heading toward the Chambers Street subway station, when her phone buzzed. A number she didn't recognize. She pressed SEND.

"It's me," Chance said.

"You got the message?"

"I did. What's it mean?"

"Not sure yet. I'm trying to find out more."

"It's something to do with down south, isn't it?"

"Maybe."

She stopped outside the subway entrance. The grate at her feet rattled as a train went by below.

"If the circumstances were otherwise," he said, "I'd say someone did us a favor."

"It could be unrelated. I'm sure he had enemies."

"You should have let me end it down there. It would have been simpler."

"Too late for that. I'm going to shake some trees, see what I can find out. How long's this number good for?"

"About five minutes. I think it's best to cut some ties. Don't take it personally."

"I won't. What are your plans?"

"I'm going to move around a little. Cleveland for a few days, then I'll catch a train."

"What direction?"

"Haven't decided."

Careful now, not wanting to tell her where he was going.

After a moment, he said, "You want me out there?"

"No. Do what you need to. I'm getting rid of this number, too. I'll give your guy the new one."

"Any shit starts to jump off about this, you need to let me know."

"I will."

"Might be a better idea if you just get out of there for a while."

"I'm thinking about it."

"I don't want to have to answer to Wayne if something happens to you over a deal I was involved with."

"He wouldn't blame you."

"I wouldn't count on that. And he has a long memory."

"You've got nothing to worry about."

"If you need me out there, call my guy. Don't screw around."

"We'll see," she said and ended the call.

She shut the phone down, pried off the back, and took out the chip. She snapped it in two with gloved fingers, flipped the pieces into a storm drain. Then she dropped the phone in a trash bin, went down into the station.

Back in the apartment, she broke open another phone, powered it up, and called Hector.

"It's me," she said. "New one."

"Got it."

She hit END, punched in Rathka's number, waited while Monique put her through.

When he came on the line, Crissa said, "Anything new from Texas?"

"I talked to our friend in Austin. He agreed to take half now, half later when he starts to show some results."

"You pay him?"

"I wired it out yesterday. One twenty-five."

"He better produce."

"He's aware of that, but he says it'll be weeks before he knows anything. January at the earliest, maybe February. Still, as I said, nothing's for certain until that board sits down in March."

"When does he want the rest?"

"I told him he'd get it when we got some proof things were moving along. Like an early letter to the board, expressing support. A declaration of intent."

"We give him the two fifty, and that hearing doesn't go our way, there'll be issues."

"He knows that. I'll give it a couple weeks into the new year, then rattle his cage a little if I haven't heard from him. But I have to be careful here. I'm putting myself at risk as well."

"I know that. I appreciate it. Listen, I may need to go away for a few days. Not sure when yet, or where. If I do, I'll get in touch, let you know where you can reach me."

"I hope that's not as ominous as it sounds. You're worrying me."

"There's nothing to worry about," she lied. "Everything's under control."

She got the suitcase from the closet, opened it on the bed, and took out the .38 and the carton of shells that had been in the safe deposit box. She broke open the cylinder, checked the loads, then closed it again. She'd have to carry it now, and that bothered her—but she couldn't take the chance of getting caught without it.

She was on the futon, a glass of wine in her hand, night creeping across the floor, when her cell began to trill. Hector.

"That guy you were asking about," he said. "Peaches."

"Yeah?"

"I made some calls. I got a number for him, or at least somebody who can reach him."

"Good, what is it?"

She took the phone into the bedroom, shooed the cat off the desk. She found a pen and wrote the number on the back of an envelope.

"Thanks," she said. "I'll let you know what happens."

"I'm headed up to my nephew's place in Newark. He knows some people around there, maybe they've heard something."

"You going tonight?"

"Might as well. I just talked to Luisa. Everything's okay. Kids think it's a little vacation, you know?"

"Good."

"If I find out anything, I'll call you."

"Thanks."

"But you need to be careful, all right? Just in case."

"I always am," she said.

TWENTY

They'd parked the El Camino on a side street, with a diagonal view of a row of old homes. Three doors from the corner was the address Stimmer had given them, a two-story house with a small yard. There were lights in the front windows. No one had come in or out in the three hours they'd been here.

"How long are we gonna wait?" Terry said.

"Long as it takes."

They were on the west side of Jersey City, new businesses and restaurants a few blocks away. Here, houses with sagging porches, sneakers hanging from telephone wires.

"What he told us," Terry said. "It could all be bullshit."

"Only one way to find out."

A shadow moved behind a window.

"Someone's in there," Eddie said.

"What about the wife and kids? He's supposed to have a wife and kids."

"I'll worry about that."

The front door opened. A Hispanic man in a green flight jacket came onto the porch, cell phone to his ear.

"Give me your phone," Eddie said.

"Why?"

"I don't want to spook him when he sees the number."

Terry handed it over. The man started up the block, still talking, then closed the phone and put it away. He went to a brown Chevy Nova, unlocked it, and got behind the wheel. They heard it start up, saw white exhaust swirl from the tailpipe.

Eddie punched in the number he'd gotten from Stimmer's cell. The driver took out his phone, looked at it. Eddie pressed END.

"That's him," he said.

The Nova pulled out, crossed the intersection in front of them.

"Follow him," Eddie said. "But stay back."

The Nova stood out in traffic, was easy to keep in sight. Suarez led them out of the city, onto the Parkway, heading north. After a while, he moved into the far right lane and signaled for the exit.

"He's taking us to Newark," Terry said.

"Don't lose him."

They left the Parkway, wound through back streets into a warehouse district. Narrow one-way streets and no other cars. They could see the Nova's taillights ahead.

"I don't like this," Terry said.

The Nova pulled up outside a tire shop.

"Drive past," Eddie said. "Don't slow down."

As they went by, he got a glimpse of open bay doors,

discarded tires. Salsa blasted from inside. He watched the shop in the rearview, saw Suarez get out of the Nova and go in.

"Make a left up here," Eddie said. "Circle around. Kill the lights."

Four left turns later, Terry pulled to the curb two blocks down from the tire shop. The streetlamp above them was out. The next one, a half block up, flickered on and off.

Light from the shop bled into the street, the music filtering down to them. Five minutes later, Suarez came out carrying an oversized gym bag, got back in the Nova.

"You think that's money?" Terry said.

The Nova pulled away from the curb.

"Turn around here," Eddie said. "I don't want to drive past there again."

Terry swung a U-turn, lights off.

"Go up a block, turn right," Eddie said. "It's dead around here at night. He'll be easy to find."

They traced a slow grid, headlights off. The warehouses and automotive shops they passed were dark. There was no sign of the Nova.

"Shit. Where'd he get to?" Terry said.

They turned onto a wide two-way street along a row of warehouses.

"Slow down," Eddie said. He looked into alleys and driveways as they crept past. Not liking it, feeling too exposed.

"We can always go back to his house," Terry said. "Wait for him."

Near the end of the block was a narrow alley between two warehouses. Eddie saw the red glow of brake lights on a brick wall.

"There he is," he said. "Keep going. Make a right here, go down a block, and pull over."

They drove past the alley, made the turn. When Terry pulled to the curb, Eddie took Stimmer's Ruger from his coat pocket.

"Wait here, keep an eye out," he said. "In case I miss him, or I have to clear out quick. If you see him drive past, follow him, see where he goes. Then come back and pick me up."

He held out the Star. Terry looked at it.

"You know how to use it, right?" Eddie said. "There's a round in the chamber already. Just point it and squeeze the trigger."

"No. I'm good."

"What are you scared of? If things jump off, you want to be out here holding nothing but your dick?"

"I'll be okay."

Eddie shook his head, handed the phone back. "Keep that on, in case I need to reach you."

He got out, tucked the Star in the back of his belt, under the sweater. The metal was cold against his skin. He kept the Ruger down at his side.

He started down the street, no cars in sight, every building dark and empty. A wide service alley ran behind the warehouses. Loading docks back here, Dumpsters, doors with security lights, alarm company signs. He counted buildings. At the fourth one, the loading gate was open enough for a man to climb under. Light from inside threw a yellow bar on the concrete dock.

He stopped one building short, staying close to the wall. The Nova was parked in the alley between the buildings, empty. Keeping an eye on the loading gate, he came up beside the car and looked inside. The bag was gone.

He waited a few moments, listening, then crossed to the loading dock. He looked under the gate, saw racks of metal shelving, boxes, an oil-stained concrete floor, fifty-five-gallon drums.

He crouched to get a better angle, saw a workbench against the far wall, a single rack of fluorescent lights above it. No one inside.

He pulled himself up onto the dock. With the Ruger in front of him, he ducked beneath the gate, stood up on the other side.

In the darkness to his right, he heard the unmistakable ratcheting of a shotgun. Knew it was pointed at his head.

"Hey, *puta*," Hector Suarez said. "Where's your partner?"

Eddie didn't move. On the floor to his left he saw the open gym bag, loose shotgun shells inside. No money.

"Drop that shit, homes," Suarez said. "Just toss it away."

"We need to talk."

"Toss it."

Eddie bent, put the Ruger on the floor.

"Now ease out of that coat. Let it fall where it is."

He shrugged out of the trench coat. It bundled at his feet.

"Walk forward. Center of the room. Safety's off on this bitch."

Eddie stepped forward, hearing Suarez behind him. There was the click of a switch, then the drone and rattle of the gate closing. He looked around. It was a big room, most of it lost in shadow. Shelves of cardboard boxes rose almost to the ceiling.

"Last time I'll ask. Where's your partner?"

"Out there somewhere. Easy, Hector. You don't know what you're dealing with here."

Suarez came around, keeping his distance. Eddie looked into the muzzle of a pistol-grip shotgun. Suarez kicked the Ruger skittering into the shadows.

"What's your name?"

"Eddie Santiago. I work for Tino Conte."

"Bullshit."

Eddie didn't respond.

"You the one that called me before?"

"I needed to be sure it was you."

"How'd you get the number?"

"How do you think? This has nothing to do with you, Hector. Don't get involved."

"I think you already got me involved, homes. Why don't you kneel down there?"

"These are new pants. "

"You think I'm fucking with you?"

Eddie knelt, felt cold concrete under his knees.

"You got a phone? To call your partner?"

"You can call him yourself. His number's in your phone."

Suarez took another step back, watching him over the barrel of the shotgun.

"Think this through, Hector. It isn't about you. It's about the money. And the woman."

"What woman?"

"Lead me to her, and there's enough cash to go around for all of us."

"Man, you don't even know what the fuck you're talking about."

Holding the shotgun one-handed, Suarez drew the cell from his jacket pocket.

"Stimmer told me everything," Eddie said. "We had a long conversation. How do you think I found you?"

"Shut up." He thumbed numbers on the phone. The shotgun didn't waver.

"That was Tino's son-in-law that got capped down there," Eddie said. "You know that, right? He wants payback. Can you blame him?"

Suarez set the phone down, stepped back. He'd put it on speaker. Eddie could hear the ringing on the other end.

Suarez pointed the shotgun at his head. "Talk to him. Tell him to come down here."

"I can't control him. He'll do what he wants."

"If he doesn't, then I'll just take you out right here, go looking for him."

The line picked up on the third ring. Silence. Eddie said, "Terry."

A pause, then, "Yeah?"

"Tell him," Suarez said.

"Come down the alley to the loading gate," Eddie said. "Fourth warehouse from the street, where the Nova's parked."

"You find him?"

"Just come down."

"Tell him I'll open the gate a little," Suarez said. "Then he's going to slide his weapon in first."

"He's not carrying."

"I don't believe that."

"What's going on?" Terry said.

"It's okay," Eddie said. "Everything's under control. We're just going to talk."

"Hey," Suarez said. "Can you hear me?"

"Who's that?"

"Man who's holding a shotgun to your partner's head."

Another pause, then, "I can hear you."

"I'm going to open the gate one foot," he said. "Whatever kind of coat you're wearing, you push it through. Then you show me your hands. Hold them out and keep them there. You got it?"

"I got it."

"You do anything besides that—or if there's more than one of you out there—I take your partner's head off."

"I understand."

"Then do it."

He picked up the phone, closed it, put it back in his jacket. "Tino's not going to like this," Eddie said.

"Fuck him. Only one person had shit to do with this. And he's dead."

"Tino's not buying that. They took a half million from that game, you know that? You get your share?"

"Man, shut up with that talk."

"There's got to be plenty left. We find it, we split it between the three of us. Tino doesn't care about the money. It's ours to keep. You lead us to the Stone woman, to Chance, we all get paid."

There was a tap at the metal gate. Suarez looked at it, backed farther toward the wall.

"Just stay right there, homes," he said to Eddie. "Don't move an inch."

With the shotgun in his right hand, he reached back with his left, found the wall switch. The gate rattled, rose up a foot, stopped.

"Throw your gun in here," he said.

"Don't have one."

"Coat."

"Hang on."

Terry's denim jacket came through the opening. Suarez crossed to the gate, watching Eddie. He picked up the jacket, then backed toward the switch again.

"You help us," Eddie said, "you'll be doing Tino a favor. Whatever your part was in this, it's forgotten. All he wants is the woman and Chance."

Suarez tossed the jacket aside. "What he wants and what he gets are two different things. Now shut up." He looked at the gate and said, "Hands."

Terry put his arms through, sleeves pushed to his elbows.

"I'm going to raise that gate again," Suarez said to him. "You squeeze through on your belly. If there's a weapon on you, I'll take you out right there. Understand?"

Terry mumbled a response.

"What?" Suarez said.

"I said I understand."

Suarez looked at Eddie, then worked the switch. The gate rattled up slowly and stopped.

"Come through," Suarez said. "Hands up in front of you."

Terry scuttled under the gate, stood, saw Eddie on his knees. Suarez turned fully toward him, aiming the shotgun with both hands.

"Easy," Suarez said. "Slow."

Terry raised his hands, came forward. Eddie looked at Suarez's back, drew the Star from under his sweater, and shot him through the left knee.

The impact blew the leg out from under him. He hit the floor, and Eddie came up fast, gripped the shotgun barrel, twisted it out of his hands. He stepped back, pointing the Star at Suarez's head.

"Jesus Christ," Terry said.

Suarez moaned. He was holding his leg with both hands, blood soaking through his pants. Eddie went around him, put the Star away, hit the wall switch. The gate slid down and shut. The motor went silent.

Suarez looked up at him, his face tight with pain. "Moth-er*fucker.*"

Eddie held the shotgun out to Terry. "Take this."

Terry hesitated.

"I said take it."

Terry took the shotgun, stepped back.

Eddie squatted, avoiding the slow pool of blood around Suarez's leg. He took Stimmer's razor from his pants pocket, opened it. Suarez looked at the blade.

"Now," Eddie said. "We talk."

TWENTY-ONE

The retirement home was in Asbury Park, twenty stories of pink concrete that looked out on trash-strewn dunes, the ocean beyond. A two-hour drive down from the city, but she'd found the address easily. Next door was the municipal sewer plant, machines chugging away in there behind high walls, the smell of it faint in the air. Out past the beach, waves splashed high around the jetties.

She parked the rental in a visitor's spot, stepped out into the wind. Scraps of newspaper blew past her. Out front, an American flag snapped on a pole.

She went up wide stone steps into a lobby that smelled of disinfectant and floor wax. A heavy black woman was at the reception desk. To the right, double doors opened onto a dining hall, the tables already set for dinner. An elderly uniformed guard sat near a bank of elevators, reading a newspaper.

Crissa was at the desk a full ten seconds before the receptionist acknowledged her. When she said who she'd come to see, she was handed a clipboard with a sign-in sheet, a pen taped to a string. Crissa made swirling marks on the signature line without forming any letters, gave it back. The woman took it, gave her a visitor's pass torn from a pad, pointed down a long hall. The security guard never looked up.

She walked past open doors, glanced into a TV room, saw half a dozen seniors sitting around, some in wheelchairs, watching a soap opera on a flat-screen set. Across the hall was an empty music room with a piano, a bouquet of artificial flowers atop it. Halfway down the corridor, a gurney was parked against the wall, the sheets rumpled and stained, restraining belts hanging loose.

The activity room was at the end of the corridor. Folding chairs and card tables, a cabinet stocked with board games. Jimmy Peaches sat in a big upholstered chair facing a window, his back to her. Beside him was an aluminum walker. He was alone in the room.

He heard her footsteps, craned his neck to look back at her.

"Jimmy," she said. "*Come sta?*"

He smiled, struggled to rise.

"Don't get up," she said.

"Come here, you. Let me get a look at you. It's been a long time."

He took her left hand in his right, pulled her close. She gave him a quick embrace, felt his frailness against her. What was left of his hair was combed straight back. He wore a pale yellow sweater over a bright white polo shirt, the initials JCF above the breast pocket. The crease on his pants was sharp, his shoes shiny.

"You look terrific," he said. "You haven't changed at all."

"You're just being a gentleman."

"No, I mean it. You haven't."

"May I sit?"

"Please. You're my guest."

She got a folding chair from one of the tables.

"You find the place all right?" he said.

"Your directions were good. Thanks for seeing me."

"I chased everybody out. I still have a little clout around here."

She pulled the chair close, sat. "So, how are you, Jimmy?"

"I woke up this morning. That's a good thing."

"You look sharp."

"I try. I was happy to hear from you. I don't get many visitors these days. Jimmy Junior used to come twice a week. He's inside now."

"I heard. I'm sorry."

"My grandson Anthony comes by when he can. He's a good kid, but he's got his own life, you know? I understand."

"I wanted to bring you something, but I wasn't sure what you could use."

"Two good legs and three feet of colon."

"Sorry. Next time, I promise."

He pointed at a glass door that led to a sunroom. "Let's talk out there," he said. "More privacy."

"You sure you're up for that?"

"I'll be okay. Just bring that thing closer, let me grab ahold of it."

She moved the walker toward him. He rose from the chair, gripped the handles, shifted his weight. She waited, ready to catch him if he lost his balance, trying not to hover.

"You'll have to get the door," he said.

"Of course." She held it open as he worked his way toward it. The tennis balls on the walker's back legs squeaked on the floor. His left leg was dragging slightly. He saw her looking.

"Stroke," he said. "Last year."

"I didn't know."

"Not such a bad one. But then, what's a good one, right?"

They went into the sunroom. Sloped floor-to-ceiling windows, wrought-iron patio furniture with green cushions. The windows were dirty, but late afternoon sun poured through, dust motes glittering in the light. The door closed behind them.

He nodded at a pair of chairs near the front windows. She followed him, keeping a half step behind. Beside the chairs was a dead fern, the soil in the planter littered with cigarette butts.

"Help comes out here to smoke," he said. "I used to sneak a cigar myself now and then, back when I could afford them."

She waited for him to sit. Instead, he leaned on the walker, looked out at the ocean. Wind was flattening the dune grass, sweeping the tops off the gray waves.

"I used to come down the Shore all the time when I was young," he said. "Asbury, Long Branch. The whole place was wide open."

He nodded to the north. "Back in the fifties, sixties, Long Branch was like the wiseguy Riviera. I was there every weekend. The Surf Lounge, the Paddock, the Piano Bar, Yvonne's Rhapsody. We owned that town. And when Monmouth Park opened for the season . . . *marone*. The whole area was crawling with guys like me."

Windblown sand rattled against the glass.

"The Harbor Island Spa was right up there on Ocean Avenue. That's where Little Pussy Russo lived. He and his brother were cat burglars, how he got the name. I used to see him around. They killed him in his apartment right there, '79, I think. It's gone now. They tore it down to build condos. Makes sense, though, right? Not something you want people to remember."

He turned toward her. "What should I call you?"

"Crissa's fine."

"That the name you gave at the desk?"

"I didn't give them anything."

"Good for you. You'll get them all talking, wondering if I have a daughter I never told them about."

"Or a girlfriend."

"Even better."

"I wouldn't put it past you."

"I wish. Come on, let's sit."

He lowered himself into a chair, one hand gripping the walker for support. She angled her chair toward his.

"What do you hear from our friend?" he said.

"Wayne sends his regards."

"I heard he was back in."

"Yes."

"That's too bad. We made a lot of money back in the nineties, the three of us. Had a good run."

"We did. You pointed us to some good work."

"You weren't much more than a kid then, but you always used this." He tapped his temple. "I was always impressed by that. When's he get out?"

"Soon, I hope. I'm working on it."

"How long's he been in?"

"Three years."

He shook his head, looked out at the ocean. "Makes you wonder if it's all worth it," he said. "This life."

"I know what you mean."

"Jimmy Junior's been in and out of the jailhouse so much, his son hardly knows him. It was the same for Jimmy, growing up. And it's my fault. I started it."

"What do you mean?"

"My old man was a tailor, up in Newark in the First Ward. Never stole a nickel in his life. Didn't like my running around the streets all day and night. Used to beat me with a barber's strop. Maybe he should have beat me harder."

"You did all right. You lived your life. You didn't let it live you."

"That the way you see it? What's important?"

"What else is there?"

"I lived my life, all right. And this is where it got me. But you didn't come down here to listen to an old man's regrets."

"I ended up in the middle of something. I thought you might be able to help."

"How?"

"Run some names by you. I know you're not calling the shots anymore—"

"I never did."

"—but I thought you might have heard some things."

"I still talk to people sometimes," he said. "I've got ears. And a few teeth left in my head. What names?"

"Louis Letteri."

He frowned. "You read about that in the papers?"

"Some of it."

"Made me angry when I heard."

She watched his eyes, wondering how much he knew, how much she should tell him. "Why?"

"This thing used to be about family, you know? Providing for them, protecting them. That's what the old-timers used to say. Now it's just about money. And staying out of jail."

"I don't understand."

"You know who his father-in-law is, right?"

"No."

"Santino Conte. Tino. Used to have all the sports betting in North Jersey. Then he got ambitious, tried to climb the ladder. He's younger than me, but not by much. Never liked him."

"Did you know Letteri?"

"No. After my time. What other names?"

"Vic Stimmer."

"Never heard of him. Jersey?"

"Staten Island. He was involved with the card game down in Florida. The one where Letteri got killed."

"Why do I think I'm not gonna like what's coming?"

She leaned closer, elbows on her thighs, hands clasped. "I was there."

"What happened?"

"Everything was under control, we were almost out. Stimmer panicked or something. Let one go."

"You knew this Stimmer from before? Worked with him?"

"Yes. Always steady, solid. I don't know what happened this time."

He shook his head slowly, looked out at the beach.

"You know more than you're telling," she said.

"When this thing happened, how did it play?"

She looked back into the activity room. A janitor was pushing a mop across the floor.

"I was out in the hallway," she said. "We were three seconds from being gone when I heard the shot."

"You had all the money already? No one got brave?"

"Right."

"So maybe he didn't panic."

"You're losing me, Jimmy."

"Like I said, I still hear things. And knowing Tino, I wouldn't be surprised."

"By what?"

"Tino and his son-in-law never got along. Everybody knew it. Lou was a big mouth. Always butting heads with Tino, with Nicky, too, the son. But Tino's hands were tied, because of the daughter. So he gave him a piece of some things he had going on in Florida, sent him down there to get rid of him."

"Okay."

"Tino's in the middle of a big case right now. RICO. Maybe twenty-five people altogether. Extortion, intent to distribute, laundering, the whole deal. If he goes down on even half of those, he's done. Now he's got health problems. Not as bad as me, but still, you don't want to be a sixty-five-year-old man going back to prison."

"I guess not."

"When you're young, it's different. It's part of the deal. You make up for it when you get out, you get new respect. But at our age, no. There's no getting out. It's where you die."

"Was Letteri part of the case?"

"Should have been, deep as he was in with Tino. But from what I hear, he wasn't indicted."

"How do you know that?"

"None of this is news. It was all in the papers. I read them every day. Guy Sterling, used to write for the *Star-Ledger*, he usually had it right, or close enough. Capeci, too, in the *Daily News*. They always had their sources."

"Guys like you?"

"Me? Never. I used to read them, though."

"So Letteri cut a deal?"

"Who knows? Tino probably thought so, paranoid as he is. Maybe he knew for sure, maybe he didn't."

"If Letteri was working with the Feds on that case, why would they leave him out there hanging? Why not stash him somewhere safe?"

"Maybe he wasn't. Maybe he was just thinking about it, or they were trying to turn him. Maybe it was all bullshit. But knowing Tino, he wouldn't want to take the chance. It's like they say, 'When in doubt, have no doubt.'"

She looked out at the beach, the waves crashing in, playing it out in her mind.

"He couldn't do it outright," she said.

"It's his son-in-law. This way, the daughter might suspect—she'd have to, with half a brain—but she doesn't know for sure. Plus it gets Tino off the hook for taking out a made guy without approval. It's all that old Sicilian bullshit. Never changes. Smile in your face, stab you in the back."

"Stimmer's dead. Someone left him in the trunk of his car."

"Up here in Jersey?"

"Yes."

"I'm not surprised."

"Why?"

"Someone kills your son-in-law, you gotta respond, right? Would look bad if he didn't. Besides, if this Stimmer pulled the trigger on Tino's say-so, he's a liability. There's only one way to make sure he keeps his mouth shut. That's the way Tino works. He's a snake. Always has been."

"That's what has me concerned."

"What?"

"What are the chances whoever took out Stimmer might be after me as well?"

"For what reason?"

"As an example. Or he's looking for the money we took from the game."

He thought about that for a moment, shook his head. "Tino would want to limit his exposure on this. The son-in-law goes, then the man who pulled the trigger goes, too. Case closed. But having someone chase around after the cash, bringing more attention? Doesn't make sense. Tino's already solved all his problems. Why complicate things?"

"Maybe he thinks Stimmer told the rest of us what his deal was."

"Why would he do that?"

"I don't know."

He shook his head again. "Like I said, makes no sense. If the man who did Stimmer is looking for you, he's got his own agenda. I don't think Tino would be happy with that."

"I see what you mean."

"If you want, I can ask around a little, on the quiet. Make a couple calls."

"I don't want to cause you any trouble."

"Like I said, I still know a few people. Give me a couple days, let me see what I find out."

"Thanks, Jimmy. I appreciate it."

"Well, you know what they say about us."

"What's that?"

"An Italian outgrows his clothes, but he never outgrows his friends."

She put a hand on his forearm, squeezed, felt the bone beneath.

"You should go away for a while," he said. "Let this play out, one way or another."

"I've thought about that."

"You should do it. If one of Tino's people is running around off the leash, causing problems, sooner or later it'll come to a head. Go somewhere safe, wait for the smoke to clear."

She nodded, stood. "Thanks for your counsel."

"Help me up."

He rose slowly from the chair. She put a hand under his elbow to guide him, braced the walker as he shifted his weight to it.

"It's almost dinnertime," he said. "I'd invite you to stay, but I don't think you'd like it much. The salisbury steak here isn't bad, believe it or not. But when they try to do Italian, forget about it. Ragu and Cheez Whiz on macaroni left over from the war."

They made their way toward the door, the janitor still in there mopping. Jimmy took her arm. "Hold on a second."

She looked at him.

"Take my advice on this if nothing else," he said. "Get

some money together. Enough to last you for a while. Go somewhere far away, somewhere warm. Wait for this to blow over."

"I don't know," she said. "This time I don't think it will."

On the way back to the city, she tried Hector. The line buzzed six times, then went to voice mail. Fifteen minutes later, she tried again. When the voice mail picked up, she said, "Me. Call back as soon as you can."

She lowered the phone, thought about what Jimmy Peaches had told her. The whole thing a setup, Tino Conte behind it, and she and Chance had walked right into it, played their parts. It made her angry at Stimmer, at herself. Wayne would have been more careful, done some digging on his own before he committed. Keep an eye out for trouble coming, he used to say, then move around it.

Too late for that, she thought. She tossed the phone onto the passenger seat. You're in the middle of it now. And the only way out is through.

TWENTY-TWO

By noon the next day, Hector hadn't called back. She paced the apartment, tried his number again. When it went to voice mail, she ended the call.

The cat watched her from the futon, sensing her agitation. She went into the kitchen, opened a can of food for it, spooned it into the plastic bowl. The sound of the electric can opener usually brought the cat running, but this time it stayed where it was. I know how you feel, Crissa thought. I don't think I could eat either.

She'd stored the .38 and the box of shells above a panel in the kitchen's drop ceiling. Now she stood on a chair and took the gun out, fit the panel back in place. She got a package of thick brown rubber bands from the desk, wrapped four of them around the .38's mother-of-pearl grips. They would steady the gun in her hand, keep it from slipping, prevent fingerprints as well.

She turned the gun over, felt its weight. She had never

fired a weapon at anyone in her life, hoped to never have to. Guns were their own craziness, like drugs. Another distraction from the real work, from the calm and careful planning that set things in motion and made them pay off. They were a necessary tool, a threat, but to be caught with one meant even more trouble. She never carried one except when working, and then got rid of it as soon as the work was done.

The .38 was different. It wasn't a tool. It was insurance.

At three in the afternoon, she tried him once more, hung up when it went to voice mail. There was nothing to do now except wait until night.

She cruised by the house twice. No lights inside. Hector's brown Nova, his latest restoration project, was parked halfway up the block. It was crooked, front wheels angled to the curb, as if it had been left in a hurry.

She parked a block away, tried his phone one last time. No answer.

She got out and walked back to the house, her right hand on the gun in her pocket. Spanish television noise blared from the house next door. On the porch, she pressed the doorbell, heard it buzz inside. She rang twice more, then went around back.

The yard was small. As she neared the door, a motion sensor light kicked on bright. She went up the wooden back steps, stood on her toes, reached and loosened the bulb with gloved fingers. The yard went dark again.

She looked through the kitchen window into darkness, listened. After a moment, she brought out the penlight and leather lockpick wallet. She thumbed the light on, held it in her teeth, took a pressure wrench and pick from their sleeves.

She worked the dead bolt first. She slid a wrench into the keyhole, twisted it to keep tension, then used the pick to rake the inside of the cylinder. When she felt the pins slip, she turned the wrench farther. The lock clicked open.

The knob was easier. When she was done, she shut the penlight off, opened the door, felt it catch against a chain. She stopped to listen again, hoping Hector wasn't inside with a gun, waiting to see who came through his back door. All she could hear was the tick of a clock in another room.

She put the pick set away, took out a small spool of heavy-gauge wire. Straightening a foot-length of it, she bent the end into a hook. She fed the wire through the gap in the door, feeling for the chain. She caught it on the second try, eased the door toward her to put slack in the links. When she pushed the wire toward the center of the door, the chain unlatched and fell free.

Drawing the .38, she moved inside, edged the door shut behind her. She raised the penlight in a reverse grip, thumbed the button.

The kitchen was small and neat, dishes stacked to dry on a counter, children's artwork on the refrigerator door. Snapshots there as well. Hector with Luisa and the kids. Hector and his brother Pablo in tuxedos, arms around each other, grinning fiercely at the camera. Hector in a wifebeater and sunglasses, arms crossed, leaning against the hood of the Nova.

She went through the dark house, fanning the penlight in front of her. In the living room, a couch, chairs, and a wide-screen TV. To the right, a staircase leading up.

Above her, floorboards squeaked.

She switched the penlight off. Another creak. Footsteps, but faint, someone trying to be quiet. She backed away from the stairs, raised the .38. She could feel her heart thumping, the blood in her ears.

Another noise above. Then someone on the stairs, coming down into darkness.

She steadied the .38 in her right hand, gripped the penlight with her left, wrists crossed, thumb on the button. Her finger tightened on the trigger. No time to cock it. To fire, she'd have to take the long double-action pull, hope she was quick enough.

Steps creaking. Midway now, a darker shape there in the shadows. Facing her.

She was squeezing the penlight button when a beam of light came from the stairs, shining fully into her face, blinding her. Her penlight clicked on, the beam reaching out, illuminating the form there, and she squeezed the trigger on the .38, the hammer coming back, the light showing her the man on the steps, the gun in his hand, and then the man was saying, "Whoa, whoa, hold on, hold on . . ." and she saw his face, eased the pressure on the trigger.

He lowered his gun, let the light drop away from her face.

"Hey, Red," Chance said. "Thought it might be you."

They were upstairs in a bedroom, the room torn apart, clothes on the floor. The mattress had been upended, a bureau turned on its side, drawers pulled out. Chance had drawn all the blinds, put a lamp on the floor, and switched it on. It threw their shadows big against the wall.

"I thought you were in Cleveland," she said.

"I lied." He sat on the edge of the box spring, put the gun down beside him. He wore a black army field jacket, a dark sweater, and black gloves. "I guess I'm getting a little para noid. Can you blame me?"

"How'd you get in?"

"Side window. You?"

"Back door." She looked around the room. "You do this?"

"Way I found it. I only got here about a half hour ago. Kids' room is the same way. Shit dumped everywhere. Somebody looking for something."

She put the .38 back in her jacket pocket. "Why are you here?"

"My guy Sladden got a call from our friend Stimmer. Or at least from someone using his cell phone. They asked for me. Thing is, when you do the math, Stimmer was already dead when the call was made."

"Then whoever killed him got his cell phone."

"And all the numbers in it. Sladden called me. He wasn't happy. He doesn't like surprises. He tried Hector a few times, yesterday and today. No answer. So I started to get worried, came up here tonight."

"You couldn't have been far."

"Wilmington. It's not Cleveland, but hey."

She knelt by the closet. Floorboards had been pried up. A battered black strongbox lay open and empty in the hole.

"Maybe they found what they were looking for," she said. She thought about the twenty thousand she'd given Hector, wondered if this was where he'd hidden it.

"Hector mixed up in anything else that might blow back on him?"

She shook her head. "He's straight. Just a go-between these days. That's all."

"That's hardly straight."

"You don't have to worry about Hector."

"Then who *do* I have to worry about?"

She looked at him.

"Nothing personal," he said, "but this thing's going farther south every day. Is there anything else you want to tell me?"

"What's that mean?"

"I don't know. He's your guy."

She shook her head in irritation. "You look through the rest of the house?"

"Yeah. Same thing. Someone took their time, didn't care about the mess they left."

She looked around the room, thinking it all through, felt his eyes on her. "His car's down the block," she said. "I'll take a look."

He got up, put the gun away. "I'll go with you."

She went first, downstairs and out the back door. They met up in the street, walked along it until they got to the Nova. She came up on the driver's side, shone the penlight in. The front seat was empty except for a folded newspaper. Nothing in the back. She tried the door. Locked.

"Back here," Chance said.

She came around, shone the light on the trunk.

"On the bumper," he said.

She guided the beam along the chrome, saw it then. Two fat blood drops, dark and dry, on the shiny metal.

Her stomach tightened. She clicked the penlight off.

"We have to look," he said.

"I know." She took out the pick set.

He turned his back, shielded her as she chose a pick and wrench. She worked by the light of the streetlamp, fit the wrench in, raked the cylinder, heard it click. The trunk lid rose slightly.

She put the pick set away, looked at the trunk, not wanting to open it.

"This is no good, being out here like this," he said. "Go on."

With the penlight in one hand, she lifted the trunk lid with the other, let the spring take it. A coppery smell drifted up, mixed with the scent of excrement. She thumbed the light on, played the beam inside.

There was a tarp there, splotched with paint and deep rust-colored stains. She picked up a corner of it, saw a pair of Timberlands.

Go ahead and look, she thought. Get it over with.

She pulled the canvas back. Hector lay on his left side, facing her. He was shirtless, his arms tied behind him. His eyes were half open, his face swollen. There was a deep cut across his throat, crusted with dried blood.

"Ah, Jesus," Chance said behind her.

She couldn't look away. There were other cuts on his chest and arms, long and deep. His pants legs were soaked through with blood.

Nausea welled inside her. She let the tarp drop back.

"We need to get out of here," Chance said.

She clicked the light off. He reached around her and shut the trunk.

He was staying in a motel near the airport. She followed him in her car. Up in the room, he locked the door, closed the curtains.

"We can't leave him there like that," she said.

He put his gun on the desk, took off his gloves and jacket.

"Nothing we can do for him now," he said. "You call the police, that starts a murder investigation. Maybe some nosy neighbor saw one of us going in there. Might be we've got a couple days grace period before they find him. Let's use it."

"He's got children. A wife. He deserves better than being left to rot in a car trunk."

"We have to look out for ourselves. He'd understand."

He crossed to the sink, ran water, palmed it into his face. He dried off with a hand towel, looked at her.

"But I guess you'll do what you want anyway," he said. "Regardless of what I say."

"That's right."

He sat on the edge of the bed. "It's just one thing after another, isn't it? This whole deal was fucked from the start."

"There's more." She told him about Jimmy Peaches, what he'd said.

"Great." He got up, started to pace. "It starts off as simple work, and now we're in the middle of a bunch of guido shit."

"Nothing for it. We are where we are."

"He's right. The best thing for both of us is to get as far away as possible."

"I have a life here," she said. "For the first time in years. I have a place I can go back to, call home. I'm not giving that up, and I'm not letting someone run me off it without a fight."

"Stimmer and Hector weren't amateurs. Whoever did this got the drop on both of them. Pretty easily, too. I don't see the sense in waiting around for him to take a crack at us."

"Do what you think is right," she said, "but I feel like I've been running my whole life, one way or another. I'm tired of it."

He leaned against the sink and crossed his arms, watching her.

"Anyway, I've got this thing down in Texas," she said. "With Wayne. I need to be in a position to handle that. I can't do it on the run."

"I know."

"There's no reason for you to stick around, though. You've got no ties here, nothing to protect."

"That's right."

"If I were you, I'd bail. Go to Cleveland, or wherever it is you were heading. If I need to reach you, I'll call Sladden."

He shook his head. "That route's gone."

"What do you mean?"

"If I walk away, I walk away. From you, from this whole mess. For safety's sake. I need to protect Sladden, too. We've all got a lot to lose."

"I understand."

"I'm sorry, Red."

"You're doing the right thing."

She opened the door and looked out into the parking lot.

A plane droned low and massive overhead, landing lights flashing.

"It was good while it lasted," he said. "We made a good team."

"We did," she said. "Be seeing you."

At a Turnpike rest stop, she found a phone booth without a security camera nearby and called 911. When the dispatcher came on, Crissa told her she'd just seen teenagers breaking into a car in Jersey City. She gave Hector's address and a description of the Nova. When the dispatcher asked her name, she hung up.

It was 3:00 A.M. by the time she got back to the city. Lionel, the night doorman, greeted her sleepily. She was feeling the leaden aftereffects of stress as she rode up in the elevator, remembering Hector's face, the marks on his body. Knowing she wouldn't be able to sleep.

At her door, she worked the key in the locks, listened for the cat. It had taken to greeting her when she came home, mewling on the other side of the door until she got it open. Silence.

When she opened the door, a cold breeze blew past her into the hall.

She stayed where she was, listening. On the wall, the alarm keypad was blinking red, waiting for the code. It hadn't been tripped.

She drew the .38, pointed it into the darkness. With her left hand, she tapped in the code. The light turned green.

The apartment was cold. She went through it with the gun up, finger tight on the trigger. The futon had been overturned, the pad slashed. The living room window was open, cold air pouring in. There was a perfect fist-sized circle cut out of the top pane near the lock, sticky remnants of tape around it. That was how they'd gotten in. The storm window had been forced up. There were shiny pry marks along its bottom edge.

In the kitchen, cabinets had been opened, pots and pans pulled out onto the floor. The refrigerator stood out crooked from the wall, door ajar. All its contents had been tipped out. On the floor, piles of sugar and flour spilled out of shattered ceramic containers. Wine bottles were broken in the sink, staining the porcelain like blood. There were footprints in the flour. Two sets. One with a sneaker pattern, a bigger one without.

She went into the bedroom. The bed had been stripped, the mattress pulled off, slashed. The closet door was thrown wide, and the maroon suitcase lay open on the floor, clothes spilling out. The lining had been cut open. The packets of money were gone.

She looked around, realized then the laptop was missing. The desk had been pulled away from the wall, the drawers taken out and dumped.

She went back into the living room, looked out the window onto the fire escape. On the outside wall, the rubber stripping that covered the alarm wiring had been peeled away. A pair of tiny alligator clips dangled from bare wire. They'd bypassed the system, done it quickly enough that no one had seen them and called the police—but they'd left quickly as well, forgotten the clips. She looked across the street. A handful of smokers stood outside the bar, puffing away in the cold.

She heard a meowing below, looked down, and saw the cat staring up at her from the fire escape, one floor down. It had fled through the open window, hidden out until they were gone. Smart.

She put the .38 atop the TV, looked around the apartment, felt the knife-edge of anger and loss, a stinging wetness in her eyes, all of it piling up on her. She thought about the laptop, the pictures of Maddie. Hector in the trunk.

All right, you bastards, she thought. You've got my attention now.

The cat appeared at the window, looked at her, then leaped down onto the floor. It brushed against her legs, hid behind her, arched its back, still freaked.

She looked out the window into the night.

You didn't find what you wanted, she thought, but you'll try again, won't you? And I'll be ready.

TWENTY-THREE

She spent the night on the futon, awake and dressed, the .38 in her lap. She'd locked the window again, patched the hole with cardboard and duct tape, but part of her was hoping they'd come back. Back up the fire escape and to the window, an easy target there against the streetlights.

Toward dawn, the cat curled beside her. She felt its warmth, its rhythmic breathing. After a while, her eyes grew heavy. She set the .38 on the floor, still in reach, and drifted into sleep.

When she woke, bright sunlight was pouring through the window. She reached out to touch the gun, make sure it was still there. The cat jumped to the floor, fled across the room to watch her from the kitchen doorway.

She sat on the edge of the futon, ran fingers through her hair, the night coming back to her. Hector's face. His throat. The realization she'd been fighting since she'd found him: that it was her fault.

In daylight, the apartment looked worse. She took the .38

with her into the bathroom, leaving it on the toilet tank while she showered. After she dressed, she cleaned up the kitchen as best she could. Then she stood on a chair and dislodged the panel in the drop ceiling. The box of shells was still there. She felt around beside it, had a moment of panic until her fingers touched metal. She drew out the key ring. Four keys, four safe deposit boxes, four banks.

She took down the box of shells and fit the panel back into place.

At nine, she called the number Jimmy Peaches had given her, his private phone.

"Are you all right?" he said.

She paused, unsure how much to tell him. "I'm okay."

"You don't sound it."

"How well do you know Tino Conte?"

"What's that mean?"

"Well enough to reach out to him?"

"Why?"

"That issue we were talking about," she said. "It got serious last night."

"How serious?"

"As serious as it gets."

He was quiet for a moment. "My advice for you is to stay as far away from him as possible."

"You said whoever was doing this had their own agenda, one Tino wouldn't like."

"So?"

"So maybe we have a mutual problem."

"No way I'm putting you in a room with that guy. Or anyone that works for him. Like I said, the man's a snake."

"I can't just sit around, waiting for someone to come at me again," she said. "Not knowing who or from what direction. Or when."

He sighed. "Okay. Forget about Tino, that's not happening. But there might be another way. Let me make a couple calls, and I'll get back to you as soon as I can. Don't do anything until you hear from me."

"I won't," she said.

In the bedroom, she got the overnight bag from the closet shelf, packed it with clothes, the box of shells. Then she walked the apartment, looking for anything else she might need. It occurred to her again how little she'd acquired in her life, how few were the things she called her own.

The cat followed her from room to room, making noise, getting underfoot. She opened a tin of cat food, spooned all of it onto a dish, then filled a bowl with fresh water. She set them down in the kitchen doorway, then sat on the futon and watched the cat while it ate.

When it was finished, she put on her leather jacket, dropped the .38 into the pocket, looked around the apartment a final time.

The cat stopped licking its paws, watched her, suspicious. She unlocked and opened the living room window, then pushed up the storm pane. Cold air flowed in. The cat backed away under a chair.

"Come on," she said. It didn't move. When she crossed the room, it backed away farther, as if it knew what was coming. She reached down, scooped it up, held it to her chest as she went to the window.

"Sorry, cat," she said. "You're back where you started."

She let it go. The cat half leaped, half fell from her arms, landed on its feet on the fire escape, turned to stare back up at her.

Don't look at me like that, Crissa thought. It was nice while it lasted, that's all. Now it's over.

She shut the window, locked it. The cat looked at her through the glass for a long moment, then turned and sprinted down the fire escape. She watched it go.

The Travel Inn was on 42nd Street, still Manhattan but close enough to the Lincoln Tunnel that she could get out of town fast. She left the rental car in a garage a block away, tipped the deskman to let her check in early.

She had lunch in the coffee shop, her first food of the day, and brought a takeout cup of tea up to her fifth-floor room. She got out the .38, checked the rounds again, then pulled a chair up to the window. The clouds were heavy with the threat of snow. She thought of the cat, out there on its own again.

She sat there sipping tea, the gun in her lap, looking out at the gray day, waiting for her phone to ring.

TWENTY-FOUR

Eddie ran the razor under the faucet, cleaning off the last of the dried blood. Water swirled faint pink into the drain. He'd wiped the blade clean after they'd left Suarez, but blood had caked on the hinge. He didn't want it to rust.

Terry had the woman's laptop open on the kitchen table, his face lit by the screen's glow. Angie stood in the doorway, watching them, chewing on a thumbnail.

"You know what you're doing with that thing?" Eddie said.

"Enough."

"What's in there?" He leaned over, drank from the faucet, then dried the razor carefully on a paper towel, closed it.

"Not much. Almost nothing on the hard drive. The trash has been emptied, and all the histories have been cleared."

"Whatever that means," Eddie said. He dropped the razor into the open gym bag at his feet, the shotgun visible. "Can you sell it, get some money?"

"Maybe. Hold on. There's some folders here with pictures."

"What pictures?"

"Some little girl."

Eddie came around behind him, looked over at Angie. She met his eyes for a moment, then turned and left the room.

"Show me," Eddie said.

Terry hit keys. A picture came up on the screen, a girl in pigtails, maybe eight, nine years old. She had reddish blond hair, was sitting on a carpeted floor in front of a Christmas tree. In the next photo, she sat on the edge of a dock, holding a child's fishing pole, the line in the water, an intent look on her face.

"Same girl in all the pictures?" Eddie said.

"Yeah." He clicked through more photos.

"Stop."

This one was a group portrait, kids sitting on the front steps of a school. The girl from the other photos was in the front row, giving the camera a wide smile. There was a school logo at the bottom of the picture.

"Two Rivers, Texas," Eddie said. "Never heard of it."

"Probably a small town."

"All these pictures, got to be someone important to her. Daughter maybe, or niece. Too young for a sister."

"Cute little girl."

"You need to find out where Two Rivers is," Eddie said. "There can't be too many of them. We lucked out here."

"Why?"

"Like I said, that kid means something to her. It's leverage."

Terry was silent.

212 | Wallace Stroby

"What?" Eddie said.

"I'm not going after some little girl."

"Who said we were? We just let her know we found the pictures. She'll get the idea. And if she bolts, we know at least one place she might turn up."

Terry hit the power button. The screen faded to black. "I don't know."

"We've come too far to back off now," Eddie said. "What's the problem? You've got nothing but paydays ahead of you. We've got twenty more coming from Tino, and who knows how much we'll get off the woman when we find her. Probably more money than you've ever seen in your life."

"I guess."

"You guess? What is it? That thing with Suarez still got you bothered?"

"I didn't expect it to go the way it did."

"Whose fault was that? He could have made it easier on himself. He chose not to. I did what I had to do."

"I know."

"Then stop acting like a bitch."

The phone in his coat pocket began to ring. He took it out, looked at the number. "It's about fucking time."

"Who is it?"

"Man with the rest of our money," Eddie said. He opened the phone. "Yeah."

"Sorry," Nicky said, "I just got your message. I got tied up with some shit. What do you need?"

"What do you think?"

"You have any trouble with that thing?"

"Nothing I couldn't handle. But there's the question of the balance."

"I hear you. Hold on."

Eddie waited, hearing muffled voices in the background. Terry was watching him.

When Nicky came back on, he said, "No problems with that. We got it. I'll call you tomorrow, tell you where to go."

"No. Let's do it tonight."

"What's the rush?"

"You've got it, right?"

"Yeah, we got it. But tonight's no good."

"Why not? The work's done. What's the issue?"

Another pause. Nicky came back on and said, "No issue. I think we can make that happen. Give me a half hour, I'll call you back, tell you where."

"Do that," Eddie said and hung up.

He zipped up the gym bag, hefted it, felt the shotgun's weight.

"Let's get out of here," he said. "Go get a decent meal. Then I've got a phone call to make."

Terry shut the laptop.

"Another thing." Eddie nodded at the hallway. "You want to keep an eye on her."

"What do you mean?"

"She makes me nervous, way she stands around, watching us. Listening all the time."

"She's just worried about me."

"Maybe so. But she doesn't like me very much, and she's seen some shit. You want to be careful around her."

"You don't have to worry about Angie."

"No," Eddie said, "but maybe you do. Women get that way sometimes. They drop a dime on you, think they're doing you a favor."

"Angie won't."

"That's right," Eddie said. "She won't."

TWENTY-FIVE

At dusk, she sat in the half-full parking lot of the Tick-Tock Diner, engine off, watching the traffic on Route 3, the lights of Manhattan in the distance. With the dark had come a light snow. The diner's Christmas lights reflected off the wet blacktop.

The man on the phone had told her five o'clock, but she'd been here since four, parked in the shadows at the far end of the lot, occasionally running the engine for heat. The .38 was beneath a newspaper on the passenger seat.

At six thirty, a new Impala glided into the lot, did a slow circuit, and parked close to the diner. The engine and headlights cut off. No one got out.

After ten minutes, the Impala's window slid down. The driver scanned the lot, looked at his watch. The window went back up.

She waited him out. Fifteen minutes later, he got out of the car, a short, heavily built man in a suit and overcoat. He looked around as he crossed the lot, hands in his pockets, and went up the flagstone steps to the diner entrance.

She put the .38 in her coat pocket, got out of the car. Through the diner windows, she could see him stop at the register and speak to the female cashier. She pointed, and he moved off.

Crissa went up the steps and inside, saw the driver turn into an alcove at the far end of the diner. She followed and came to a short hallway with a pay phone, MEN and WOMEN doors facing each other. She gave it a moment, waiting for someone to come in or out, then pushed open the MEN door. No one at the urinals. In the mirror, she could see the driver standing in a stall, the door open. All the other stalls were empty. He flushed, zipped up.

She came up behind him, put the muzzle of the .38 to the back of his head, crowded him into the stall. She pushed the door shut behind her, bolted it.

"Easy with that thing," he said.

She reached around, felt under his suit jacket. "What's your name?"

"This could get a little embarrassing, don't you think? We were supposed to talk in the car."

She drew a small automatic from his belt.

"What's this for?" she said.

"Hey, I don't know who you are. Better safe, right?"

Her thumb found the magazine release. She held the gun over the toilet and shook it. The clip slid out, splashed into the water.

"I really wish you hadn't done that," he said.

She put the gun in her pocket.

"What's your name?" she said again.

When he didn't answer, she cocked the .38, felt him stiffen.

"Be careful with that," he said.

"Name."

"Carmine."

"You alone, Carmine?"

"What do you think? I was sitting on my ass out there for a half hour. You had to be watching."

They heard the men's room door open. She screwed the muzzle of the .38 into his scalp. Someone used a urinal, whistling softly to himself. He flushed, ran water in the sink, and then they heard the rattle of the towel dispenser. The door opened and closed again.

"You're starting to piss me off," he said. "I'm here as a favor. Take that thing away from my head, before I take it away from you."

"Tough guy, huh?"

"Try me."

She lowered the gun.

"I don't know who you are either," she said. "Or who you work for. Better safe, right?"

"I'm here as a gesture to our friend down the Shore. That's all. You understand that?"

"Yes."

"Then don't make me regret it."

"What do you have to tell me?"

"This is the only time we're ever going to meet. So stop busting my balls and listen up. I'm not repeating shit."

She decocked the .38. "Go on."

"There's a guy used to work for Tino, just got out of Rahway.

His name's Eddie Santiago. They call him Eddie the Saint. He was Tino's go-to guy when the old man had to make a move and didn't have enough muscle."

"So?"

"So Eddie's back in the fold. He's the guy that took out your two partners."

"How do you know that?"

"Word gets around. He's *matto*, crazy. No one wants anything to do with him. Sometimes he runs with a punk kid named Terry Trudeau. A burglar."

She remembered the alligator clips on the alarm wire.

"Where do I find them?" she said.

"You're on your own with that. Tino hangs at a market sometimes, up in Irvington. He keeps an office in the back. Eddie, who knows?"

"Why are you telling me all this?"

"Like I said, for our friend. He has some favors due."

"You work for Tino?"

"That prick? Never."

"Who do you work for?"

"The pope. How long are we going to stay in here?"

She put the .38 away, reached back and unbolted the stall door.

"Wait here five minutes," she said. "Then go out to the counter, order a cup of coffee, sit there and drink it. I'll be able to see you through the window. If you come out and try to follow me, you won't give me any choice. You know that, right?"

"Got it." He snapped his gum. "Coffee. Right."

She backed out of the stall, let the door swing shut. He

stayed where he was. She took out his gun, dropped it into the trash can by the door, went back into the diner and toward the exit, not walking fast, not looking back.

In the parking lot, she knelt by the Impala, Christmas lights bathing it in red and green. She took out her pocket knife, sank the tip into the right rear tire. Air hissed out.

She did the same to the right front, the Impala's springs creaking as it sank lower, settled crookedly. She looked back at the diner windows. He hadn't come out.

She closed the knife and walked back to her car.

The phone woke her.

She looked at the nightstand clock—10:00 P.M. She'd fallen asleep fully dressed on the bed, the phone beside her.

It trilled again. Hector's number. She hit SEND, lifted it to her ear.

Silence. Then a man's voice said, "I know you're there. I can hear you breathing."

She waited.

"We should talk," he said. "Before all this gets out of control."

"Talk about what?"

"What you've got. What I want. What I'll do to get it. It's not too late to work it out."

"How will we do that?"

"Simple. Give me the money you took from the card game. All of it."

"What card game?"

"Don't. You didn't get where you are by being stupid, did

you? Don't start now. You're going to come out ahead any-way, right?"

"How's that?"

"You'll be alive."

When she didn't respond, he said, "That's good. You're thinking."

"I am. Maybe I know a couple things about you, too."

"Good for you. Like I said, we'll keep it simple. We agree on a figure, you hand it over. You go steal some more from someone else. All there is to it."

"That easy, is it?"

"Just that easy. I'm going to call you back tomorrow, and then I'm going to tell you where and when we're going to meet."

"Oh, we'll definitely meet," she said. "I guarantee that."

"Don't get ahead of yourself. Been to Texas lately?"

She felt her arms grow cold.

"What do you mean?"

"Cute little girl. She yours?"

The laptop, she thought. The photos. It had been stupid to leave them on there.

"Still there?" he said.

She took a breath, let it out slow. "I don't know what you're talking about."

"Elktail Elementary, that a good school? Two Rivers, Texas. I looked at a map. What is that, a couple days' drive? Maybe two hours on a plane?"

"What do you want?"

"I want you to stop fucking around. I did two of your partners. You doubt my seriousness?"

She thought of Hector in the trunk, what they'd done to him.

"Way I see it, there's an easy way and a hard way," he said. "Easy way is to get all that cash together and give it to me, then walk away. We do it the hard way, I'm not responsible for the consequences."

"I think you've gotten some bad information."

"Stimmer told me you took more than four hundred out of that game. Maybe you spent some of it, but that still leaves both of you with close to two hundred K apiece, right?"

"There was never that much."

"No? Your buddy Hector seemed to think that was a good guess. He held out for a while, loyalty and all that, but he wouldn't shut up near the end. You'd be surprised what people tell you if they think there's even the slightest chance you'll let them live."

"You're a sick fuck, aren't you?"

"Maybe tonight I'll be a sick fuck on my way to Texas. What are you going to do, hide her somewhere for the rest of her life? I find her and then our negotiations change, don't they? Two hundred won't be enough. Seems to me I'm giving you the easy way out."

She looked out the window. Snow had begun to blow against the glass.

"Skull it out as much as you want," he said, "but there's only one way you'll get rid of me. Give me the money and write it off to experience. Look at all the angles. It's the only way out." The line went dead.

She sat on the bed, could feel her heart in her chest. She started to punch in Leah's number, stopped. Better to use a pay phone. If he somehow got this phone from her, the number would be in there. It would be a place to start.

Even the money wouldn't be enough, she knew. Once she gave him the cash, however much, she'd be dead. He couldn't take the risk. Wouldn't leave her out there, alive, trying to figure out a way to get it back.

TWENTY-SIX

They sat in the El Camino, lights and engine off, looking out into the wrecking yard. They were back in Carteret, less than a half mile from Casco's place, off a long strip of road lined with auto body shops and salvage yards.

"What'd she say?" Terry said.

"A lot of bullshit, but she'll come around. Your hands shaking?"

"I'm just cold." Flecks of snow settled on the windshield, melted. "Where is he?"

"He'll be here." Eddie looked at his watch. "It's only eleven."

The gate had been left open for them, but the office windows were dark. The yard was lit by vapor lamps on high poles. They'd parked in the shadow of the building, twenty feet in from the road.

Ahead of them were stacked rows of crushed cars, a burned-out Good Humor truck up on blocks, hood open and engine missing. Beyond it, a high chain-link fence strung with barbed wire.

"How come we didn't go to the market, like last time?" Terry said

"The old man doesn't like to handle money. Won't be anywhere around it. That's why he's sending the kid."

"You trust him?"

"Tino doesn't have the balls to screw with me, and Nicky doesn't take a piss unless his father gives the okay. There's nothing to worry about."

"Then why'd you bring that?" He nodded at the half-open gym bag at Eddie's feet, the shotgun and Stimmer's Ruger inside.

"You never know, right?"

They sat in silence for a while. Then Terry said, "I need to ask you something."

"What?"

"Are you serious? About the Texas thing?"

"She thinks we are. That's what's important. She's not stupid. She'll deal. But if we have to go down there, we will."

Terry began to tap his foot on the floorboard.

"You cranked?" Eddie said.

"I told you. I haven't touched that shit since you've been out."

"So I'm a positive influence."

"I just don't like this. I don't like being here."

"Twenty grand is twenty grand," Eddie said.

"Is it worth it?"

"What?"

"The things we've done. Is the money worth it?"

"Up to you, isn't it? How much is enough? Fifty grand, a hundred?"

"What do you mean?"

"You think I've gone through all this for the crumbs Tino throws me? I'm building a nest egg here. You, too. We find that woman, one way or another, take whatever she has left. Maybe she leads us to the partner. And knowing what I know about Tino, the shit he pulled, I can shake some more loose from him, too. Maybe a lot more."

"I don't understand."

"Think about it. Tino wants his son-in-law gone. He gets Stimmer to do it for him. Then he gets us to do Stimmer. Makes sense, right? That's why he wanted it done quick, before Stimmer started talking."

"The money we found in his place . . ."

"Probably what was left of the cash he got up front. I'm guessing Tino suckered him into coming back up here to get the rest. He should have stayed in Florida. He'd still be alive."

"Shit. I had no idea."

"You surprised?" Eddie said. "Way of the world. Everybody's looking out for themselves."

"I didn't think I'd be in this deep, you know? All the shit that's been happening. It was never like this before."

"Losing your nerve?"

"I didn't say that."

"The way you creeped Stimmer's place, that woman's? You're a natural. You've got skills. It's like they say, find your place in life and everything gets easier, makes more sense."

"I'm not so sure."

"What did you have before I got out? Nothing. Not even a

job. Now you've got money in your pocket, more coming in. What's the issue?"

"I'm just tired of living like this. Having a knot in my stomach all the time."

Eddie looked at him. "You blame me for that?"

"I didn't say that."

"You want to go home to the little woman every night? Be a daddy? Join the Elks? Little late for that, isn't it?"

"Maybe not." Terry couldn't look at him.

"Now you're just pissing me off. You want that life? What have you done to deserve it? You're just like me. Why should you get something I can't?"

"That's not what I meant."

"I know what you meant. Enough with that shit already."

Eddie looked at his watch again. Eleven twenty.

"Come on," he said. "Let's take a look around."

They got out, light snow blowing around them. Eddie took the Star from his belt, held it at his side. To their right, toward the fence, was a double row of newer wrecks parked nose to nose. Smashed front ends, twisted metal, and spiderwebbed safety glass. On the inside of one windshield was a rust-colored starburst pattern. Blood.

"Creeps me out," Terry said.

"What?"

"Those cars. Knowing people died in them."

"We all have our time. No one one gets to pick when."

They walked past piles of rusted auto parts, engine blocks, listened to the wind.

"If someone's out here," Eddie said, "he's freezing his ass off."

They did a circuit of the yard, then went back to the El Camino, saw headlights on the road. The lights slowed.

"Here he is," Eddie said. He put the Star in his coat pocket.

The green Mercury turned into the lot and pulled abreast of them, Nicky at the wheel. He looked over at Eddie, raised his chin in greeting, doused the headlights, left the engine running.

"It's just him," Terry said. "That's good, right?"

Nicky got out, left the door open. He wore a long leather coat over a suit. "Hey," he said. He went around, opened the trunk, took out a package the size of a shoe box, wrapped in butcher paper.

"Just so you know." He shut the trunk lid. "My father threw in another ten, show his gratitude."

"Generous of him," Eddie said. Neither of them moved. Snow drifted in the air.

"Colder than a motherfucker tonight," Nicky said. "You going to take this or what?"

"Why so nervous, Nicky?"

"I'm not nervous. Just freezing my balls off. I want to get out of here."

"Step away from the car."

"Come on, no bullshit." He held the package out. "I need to get going. I got a date."

Wind ruffled Eddie's coat. He put his hands in his pockets.

"We going to stand out here all night?" Nicky said. "Shit, *somebody* take it."

The side window of the El Camino exploded. Eddie saw the flash, heard the flat crack of the rifle. He shoved Terry away, said, "Get down," and drew the Star.

Nicky dropped the package. Eddie fired at him. There was another crack, and a round punched into the El Camino's right front fender. Air hissed from the tire. Eddie tracked the flash this time, the top of the Good Humor truck, fired twice at it. The first round sparked off the front of the truck. The second *whanged* through the empty interior.

More rifle shots, sounding almost as one. The El Camino's windshield imploded. Eddie kept firing, hot casings flying past him, until the slide locked back.

A shadow rolled from the roof of the truck, hit the ground. A man got to his feet and ran toward the fence, a limping stride that favored one leg.

Eddie pulled open the passenger door of the El Camino, tossed the empty Star inside, drew the shotgun from the gym bag. The seat and dashboard were covered with cubes of safety glass.

Nicky lay facedown by the Mercury's open door, not moving. Eddie went past him. The running man was almost to the fence, the limp slowing him. Eddie fired, the shotgun kicking back harder than he'd expected. He knew the shot spread would be too wide at this range to bring down a man. He pumped another round into the chamber, went after him.

The man reached the fence, leaped and caught the chain links, started to climb, full in the light now. It was Vincent Rio. He wore a quilted black jacket, black jeans, work boots.

Eddie walked toward the fence. Rio was grunting with effort, the wide boots slipping from the chain links. He reached the top, slung a leg over, caught his jacket on the barbed wire. He pulled at it, nylon ripping, got the other leg up. The barbs snagged his clothes in a half-dozen places, held him there, the fence rattling with his struggles. Snow drifted past the vapor light above him.

Eddie reached the fence, looked up at him.

"Wait a minute!" Rio said. "Just wait one goddamn—"

Eddie fired, felt the recoil, pumped, fired again. Bits of cotton insulation drifted in the air, were scattered by the wind.

He walked back to the Good Humor truck, climbed on the back bumper. There was an AR-15 on the roof, spent cartridges scattered around it.

He left it there, went back to the El Camino. Terry was out of sight. Nicky hadn't moved. White exhaust puffed from the Mercury's tailpipe.

"Come on out, kid," he said. "It's done." There was no answer.

He walked around the rear of the El Camino. Terry sat on the ground, leaning against the bumper, his left hand inside his leather jacket. His face was pale.

"Shit," Eddie said. He knelt beside him, set the shotgun on the ground. "Move your hand. Let me see."

Terry took his hand away, the palm red with blood. Eddie unzipped his jacket the rest of the way. He could see where the round had gone in, just above the belt on the left side.

"Is it bad?" Terry said.

"Yeah, it's bad."

"You need to call an ambulance."

Eddie sat back on his haunches. "Can you stand?"

Terry shook his head. "I can't move my legs."

Eddie stood, went over and picked up the package. He took out the razor, slashed through the paper and string.

"Eddie . . ."

Inside the box were three stacks of money wrapped with rubber bands, twenties on top. He thumbed the bills. After the first three twenties in each stack, it was all white paper.

"Son of a bitch." He pulled the twenties free, dropped the box. One of the rubber bands broke, and the wind blew white paper along the ground. He folded the real bills into his pants pocket.

"Eddie, you gotta help me."

He got the gym bag from the El Camino, put the empty Star inside. The windshield had a fist-sized hole, the glass sagging inward. The floor was littered with broken glass and foam rubber blown from the seat backs.

He carried the bag back to Terry, set it down, squatted again.

"It feels like it went all the way through," Terry said, his voice weaker, his forehead filmed with sweat. "I'll be all right if I get to a hospital."

"You're bleeding like a bitch, kid. No way I can drive you anywhere, not get blood all over the place."

"Then call an ambulance." His breathing was shallow now, faster. "Call 911 . . . tell them where I am. "

Eddie shook his head.

"Please, Eddie. I won't say anything to anybody. I swear."

Eddie slid the shotgun into the bag, took out the Ruger.

"Call Angie. She'll come. She'll take care of me. You don't have to stay . . ." He saw the gun then. "What are you doing?"

"I'm sorry about this, kid. I really am."

"Eddie, don't . . ."

"Close your eyes."

Snow drifted down around them, flakes settling in Terry's hair. Eddie stood.

"Eddie, please. Call Angie. I won't tell anybody anything."

"You'll talk, kid. You know you will. You'll be so doped up, you won't even know what you're saying."

"Eddie, not like this . . ."

"Don't be scared."

Tears were streaming down Terry's face. He closed his eyes, sobbing silently. Eddie fired once.

The wind picked up, howled through the yard. He put the Ruger in his coat pocket, zipped up the gym bag. He carried it to the Mercury, stepped over Nicky's body, reached in and popped the trunk latch. He put the bag in the trunk, shut the lid, got behind the wheel.

It was still warm in the car, the vents humming. He swung around in a three-point turn, felt Nicky's legs crunch beneath the tires. He didn't look at the El Camino as he went past.

When he reached the road, he turned left, switched on the headlights. A half mile later, he got on the Turnpike, headed south. He found himself speeding, had to will himself to slow down. Snow flitted in the headlights, the white line blurring, the road disappearing beneath his wheels.

He knocked twice on the door, waited. Knocked again hard, gloved fist against wood.

Footsteps inside the house.

"Open the door," he said.

"Who is it?"

"It's Eddie. I need to talk with you."

"Where's Terry?"

"That's what I need to talk to you about. Open the door."

"Is he hurt?"

"Let me in and we'll talk. I can't stand out here like this."

He heard locks being undone. The door opened a crack, the gap spanned by a chain. Angie looked out.

"What happened?"

"Come on, Angie. Let me in."

She closed the door, slipped the chain. When she opened it again, she said, "Did something happen? Where's Terry?" She was wearing a white bathrobe, her hair tied back. She kept one arm across her stomach.

"I just left him," he said. "He asked me to come see you."

"Where is he?"

"That computer, is it still here?"

"In the kitchen. Why?"

"Get it for me, will you?"

She bit a thumbnail.

"He needs it," he said. "Now."

She nodded, turned. He shut the door behind him, took out the Ruger, and shot her in the back of the head.

The laptop was on the kitchen table. He searched the house, found ten thousand in banded bills in a shoe box in the bedroom closet. Stupid kid, he thought. Left it sitting there where anyone could find it. He filled his coat pockets with cash.

The laptop under his arm, he went back out into the night.

TWENTY-SEVEN

Eddie knelt in cold, dead leaves, watching Tino's house. The other yards he'd crossed had low wooden fences or bare hedges. Tino's fence was head high, chain link. Eddie waited beside it.

Inside the glassed-in back porch was the glow of a cigarette, the silhouette of a man sitting there. The light over the porch illuminated a flagstone patio with a wrought-iron table and chairs, all dusted with snow. The rest of the yard was in darkness.

As Eddie watched, the man rose, opened the porch door, flicked the cigarette out into the yard. Then he turned and went through into the house.

Eddie gripped the chain link with gloved hands, went up the fence fast and quiet. He lowered himself down the other side, dropped to frozen earth, moved into the darkness. Beyond the patio was a pair of fig trees wrapped in canvas. He stepped behind them. The sky was clearing, the moon coming out.

After a few minutes, the man came back out, reclaimed his seat. Eddie saw the flare of a lighter, then the glow of another cigarette. He reached down, felt around until his fingers closed on a smooth stone the size of an egg. He sidearmed it into the darkness, heard it clatter against the fence.

The door opened again, and the man stepped out into the light. He was big, dark hair slicked back. He held an automatic at his side.

He tossed the cigarette and came out into the yard, frost crackling under his shoes. He seemed to look right at Eddie, then walked past him to the fence. Eddie came out from behind the trees, touched the muzzle of the Ruger to the back of his neck.

"Not a sound," he said. "I've got no issue with you. Just take it easy and you'll walk away from this."

He reached around with his free hand, took the man's gun. It was a Mini Glock. He put it in his own pocket, guided the man deeper into the shadows.

"Kneel."

When he didn't move, Eddie thumbed back the Ruger's hammer.

"You won't have time to yell. If you open your mouth, your brains will be in the trees. And whoever comes out that door next will be as dead as you are. Now kneel."

Slowly, he lowered himself to his knees, hands at shoulder height.

Eddie leaned close to him. "Who's in there besides Tino? How many others?"

"No one." Lying.

"I just want to talk to him. Get some things straightened out. No one's gonna get hurt. Is his wife in there with him?"

"No."

"Who else?"

The man exhaled, his breath frosting. "Just one guy."

"Where is he?"

"With Tino, in the kitchen."

He decocked the Ruger, put it away.

"What are they doing?"

"Waiting for a phone call."

"From Nicky?"

"Yeah."

Eddie locked a forearm across the man's throat, pulled back hard to cut off the noise. He cupped the back of his head with his other hand, pushed forward, bore the man down to the ground. He held him while he fought. Eventually the struggles slowed and stopped.

Eddie left him there, drew the Glock. He crossed the yard and went onto the porch. The door there led into a paneled hallway, family pictures on the wall. To the right, a kitchen entrance. Tino sat at the table, his back to the door, playing cards with another man. There was a cell phone and a revolver on the table.

Eddie stepped into the kitchen, said, "Hey, Tino."

The other man saw him, reached for the gun. Eddie shot him, and he went over backward in the chair. Blood spattered the cards.

Tino turned to look at him. He wore a dressing gown over an open shirt. His skin was yellowish in the kitchen light.

Eddie came around the table, pulled out a chair, sat down. They faced each other. Eddie could hear his labored breathing.

Tino said, "Nick?"

Eddie shook his head. Tino closed his eyes for a moment. When he opened them again, they were moist.

"You knew this day would come, didn't you?" Eddie said.

"You son of a bitch, just do what you—"

Eddie raised the Glock above the level of the table, fired twice. The sound of the shots echoed through the empty house.

He sat there for a while, then stood, looked at the old man still and silent on the floor. Then he went back through the porch and out into the cold night. The big man lay where he'd left him. Eddie dropped the Glock beside him.

He climbed the fence again, not caring about noise now. By the light of the moon, he made his way back to the car.

Back in the motel, he sat on the edge of the bed with his head in his hands. He reeked of gunpowder. His arms and legs felt like lead weights.

Suarez's cell phone was on the nightstand. He picked it up, saw the MISSED CALL icon. The woman's number. No message.

He slipped out of his coat, peeled off the gloves, picked up the phone, hit the RETURN CALL key. Two buzzes and the line was picked up. He listened, said nothing.

"I've been thinking about those angles," the woman said. "The best I can do is a hundred."

"Not good enough."

"It'll have to be. It's all I've got in cash."

"What about Chance?"

"He's in the wind. A thousand miles away from here by now, if he's smart. I have no way of reaching him."

"A hundred isn't enough."

"Listen to me," she said. "My split was two hundred and nine. If you talked to Stimmer—"

"Oh, I talked to him all right."

"—then you know that figure's accurate. Most of it went into an investment firm I use. Some went into bonds and notes I can't touch for months. There were other expenses, too. That left a hundred in cash. That's all I have."

A hundred thousand, plus what he already had. It would be enough to get him clear. He could head south maybe, Florida, or west to Arizona or California. Or he could get the woman to tell him where Chance was, hope he had more. The thought of it made him tired. He rubbed his eyes.

"You there?" she said.

"I'm here. Somebody like you, you probably have money stashed all over."

"Not anymore."

"The hundred, you have it with you?"

"I have to get it. It's hidden."

"Where?"

"At a place I sometimes use. About two hours from here."

"Where?"

A pause, then, "Connecticut."

"You go get it, bring it back. Call me."

"No," she said. "I'm not coming back. You meet me there, I hand you the cash, or tell you where to find it. You get it and we're done."

"You're not in a position to deal. And believe me, bitch, after tonight I've got nothing to lose."

"What's that mean?"

"You want to keep screwing around? Fine. I'll find you eventually, get that money anyway. And you'll be begging for a bullet."

"I can't come back. I'm heading north. My plan was to stop, pick up the cash, keep going."

Heading for Canada, he thought, and stupid enough to think she'll make it.

"Where are you now?" he said.

"In the city. I can't get at the money until tomorrow."

"Why not?"

"It's in the middle of nowhere. I wouldn't be able to find it at night."

"That story's almost stupid enough to be true. Here's the deal. If we meet and you don't have it, or it's not as much as you say—or there's some other bullshit excuse you come up with—then we're going to have a long talk. And if you're not there, I'm going to track you down. You know that, right?"

"I know that."

"And I might need to make that trip to Texas."

Silence on the line.

"I'll call you tomorrow," she said. "Tell you where, when."

"Tell me now."

"No. I'll call you when I have it. I'll give you time to get up there, then I'll meet you around dusk. I give you the money and then you get the fuck out of my life."

"That'll be the luckiest day you ever had, woman," he said.

"The day you see me walking away from you, and you're still breathing."

"Whatever."

"And you better pray," he said, "that you never see me again."

When the line went dead, she put on her jacket, the .38 in the pocket, left the hotel. Earlier in the evening, she'd called Leah, spent five minutes on the phone with her, then ten more with an angry Earl. She couldn't blame him. They would be more careful now, though, keep a closer eye on Maddie, watch out for strangers. She'd given them as few details as possible, but it had been enough.

It had started to snow again. She walked west on 42nd, crossed Twelfth Avenue to the Circle Line pier. A tugboat was pulling up, engine chugging, green and red running lights reflected in the water. A pair of gulls followed it, swooping in and out of the pole lights on the dock. Across the river, she could see headlights moving along the Palisades Parkway.

She took the cell from her pocket, scaled it out over the rocks and into the darkness, heard it splash. A gull swooped down, circled where it had gone in, then banked away, disappointed.

Any more contact would be on her terms now. She'd buy another phone tomorrow, make the call. Stall as long as she could, until she had a plan.

She stood there for a while, watching snow fall on the river. Then she walked back to the hotel, her hand on the gun.

TWENTY-EIGHT

When the woman answered the phone, Crissa said, "I have a message for Sladden."

"There's nobody by that name here."

She was standing at the window, looking out on 42nd Street. It had stopped snowing during the night, and the streets were clear again. She'd heard the plows rumbling by as she lay in bed, sleepless.

"He knows me," she said. "Take down this number. Tell him I'm trying to contact our mutual friend."

"I'm sorry. I can't help you with that."

"Just take the number. It's a new one he doesn't have." She read it off.

"You're wasting your time."

"I know," Crissa said. "Just humor me." The woman hung up.

She spread a towel on the desk, opened the tin of gun oil

she'd bought. She unloaded the .38, oiled it until the action worked smoothly. Then she set the shells nose up on the desk, opened her pocket knife. She laid the blade across the tips, used the gun butt to tap *X*'s into the soft lead. Scored like that, the slugs would expand when they hit, increase the stopping power. She spilled more shells from the box, did the same to them.

As she was reloading, the phone buzzed. A number she didn't recognize. When she answered, a man said, "Who is this?"

"Someone on the East Coast."

"How's that?"

"I told our mutual friend I wouldn't contact him again. But things have changed."

"None of this means anything to me, lady."

"Tell him if he doesn't call back, I understand. But if it wasn't serious, I wouldn't call."

"I'm hanging up now. Don't call this number again." The line went dead.

An hour later, she was having lunch in the hotel coffee shop when the phone began to buzz. Another number she didn't know, an area code she couldn't place.

She hit SEND, brought the phone to her ear.

"Okay, Red," Chance said. "Talk to me."

When she pulled into the Turnpike rest area, Chance was at the far end of the lot, leaning on the fender of a dark blue Mustang. He wore the same field jacket she'd seen him in last, gloves. He had his arms folded, watching her. Behind him, a line of semis queued up at the gas pumps. Traffic rushed by on the roadway beyond.

She pulled the rental up beside him. He got in.

"After the other night," she said, "I thought there was a good chance I'd never see you again."

"Me, too. But I kept thinking how Wayne would have my ass if anything happened to you."

"It's not me I'm worried about."

"You think this guy's serious? About Texas?"

"I can't take the chance he is. This needs to end." She looked over at the Mustang. "Where'd you'd boost that?"

"It's not boosted. All legal. In my name, too. This a rental?"

"Yeah."

"We need another car."

"That's our next stop."

"I've got tools if you need them."

"Good."

He looked at her. "You sure about all this?"

"I've thought it over. It's the only way."

"I don't know. This guy's already got two bodies on him, maybe more. No way he'd make any deal that leaves you alive afterward. And he's got to know that you know that."

"You're right."

"So why would he go along with you, take the bait?"

"Way I look at it," she said, "he doesn't have a choice."

———

She returned the rental at the airport office, rode with Chance over to the long-term lot. He dropped her outside the gate and drove on.

She walked the rows until she found what she wanted, an older-model Toyota Camry with smoked windows. It was a car she was familiar with, reliable and innocuous.

She took out a small rubber doorstop, wedged it between the driver's side window and door. It gave her room to work. She pulled Chance's Slim Jim from her belt, slid it down past the weather stripping and into the door. It took her two sweeps to find the control rod. She pulled up, heard the mechanism unlock.

She slid behind the wheel, took out the rest of Chance's tools, and spent five minutes working on the steering column. He'd given her a roll of black electrician's tape as well, and she used that to braid wires, then jammed a short-handled screwdriver into the ignition, twisted it. The engine came to life. She gave it gas until it was running smoothly.

The windows were iced over, so she had to run the defroster for a while. While she was waiting, she flipped the visors. The automated parking ticket fluttered down to the seat. She was in luck. The car had come in the day before. It might be weeks before anyone came to claim it.

When the windshield was clear, she backed out, drove to the gate. At the exit booth she handed over the ticket, gave the clerk ten dollars and a smile, and pulled out of the lot.

They met up at the rest stop again an hour later. He got in, looked at the steering column.

"Nice job," he said.

She handed him a folded piece of paper. "Directions. In case we get separated."

He took them. "When are you going to make that call?"

"Soon as we get up there, get settled. Have I told you how glad I am you're here?"

"Partly my fault we're in this in the first place."

"Where were you when Sladden called?"

"Philly."

"I would have figured South America, the way you were talking."

"Like I said, I had a bad feeling. Thought I'd better stay close."

"It's not too late," she said. "You can still change your mind."

He squinted, scratched his jaw. "Cold in Cleveland."

"Cold here."

"Yeah, but it'll always be in the back of my mind this guy's out there, running around loose. Better to deal with it now, I guess. Cleveland can wait."

Eddie sat on the motel bed, fed shells into the shotgun. He pumped it once to chamber a round, pushed in another to replace it. He slipped the safety on, set the gun on the bed.

He'd slept less than a hour all night, and he could feel swollen veins in his temples, tightness in his neck and shoulders. His eyes stung.

The cell phone was on the desk, next to the canvas duffel bag he'd bought. He'd gotten all his money together, added what he'd taken from Terry's place. He wasn't coming back here. When he was done with the woman, he'd head south, figure out his next move. Get clear of New Jersey before Tino's people got organized enough to look for him.

He pushed the laptop into the duffel, put clothes on top of it. It might be useful somewhere down the line. He pulled the drawstring tight.

The razor went into his front pants pocket, the shotgun into the gym bag, along with the loose shells and Stimmer's Ruger. He put on his trench coat, dropped the reloaded Star in the right-hand pocket, Suarez's cell in the left. For the first time, he noticed the brown spots that dotted the side of the coat. Terry's blood.

He wet a thumb, rubbed at them. It didn't do any good.

TWENTY-NINE

The snow had been heavier up here, and it crunched under the tires as she drove the Camry up the driveway and parked in front of the garage. They'd left the Mustang about a mile away, in the lot of a recreation area, with a half-dozen other cars.

The light was fading, the moon already visible through the clouds. They looked at the dark house.

"You sure this is all right?" Chance said.

"Caretaker comes by occasionally, but the owners are out of the country."

"What if that real estate agent decides to hold an open house tomorrow?"

"Let's hope she doesn't."

He got out, worked the turn latch on the garage door, heaved it up and open. There was a cleared space inside, oil stains on the concrete floor, cardboard boxes against the wall, a lawn mower. She drove the Camry into the garage, twisted the screwdriver to kill the engine.

Chance had a flashlight out, was playing the beam around the inside of the garage. She got out, opened the trunk, unzipped the overnight bag that was in there. She took out the .38 and the box of shells. Beneath them were banded stacks of cash. She'd emptied one of her safe deposit boxes that afternoon.

"How much is in there?" he said.

"Ten thousand. He may call our bluff, want to see some money. We'll need something to show him."

"I don't know," he said. "I think first clear shot we get at him we should take it."

"If we do and miss, and he rabbits, we may not get the chance again. We have to be sure."

The gun went into her right-hand pocket, the rest of the loose shells into her left. She zipped the bag up, shut the lid.

"We'll leave the garage open," she said. "I want him to be able to see the car, know I'm here."

She looked out on the stretch of snow-covered yard, the skeletal trees, the woods beyond already deep in shadow.

"We'll have to be careful of tracks," she said. "Try to walk where I do."

The porch door was easy. She worked the tip of her pocketknife into the mechanism, popped it, then used the blade to flip open the hook-and-eye latch. At the back door, she got her pick set out, said, "Give me some light." He shone the flashlight beam on the door as she worked the dead bolt and knob. Both locks were stiff with cold, and she had to go easy, not wanting to snap off the thin tension wrench. When she got the door open, they went into the darkened kitchen, kicked snow from their boots.

"Power?" he said.

"Yes, but be careful what you turn on."

She walked around the house. Nothing was changed since last she'd been here. It was the same upstairs. From the back bedroom, she looked down on the driveway, garage, and woods.

When she went back down, Chance had switched on a light above the stove. It lit half the kitchen. He sat at the table, a black automatic in his hands, ejected the clip, and thumbed the shells out. He pressed them back into the magazine one by one, checking the spring pressure.

She went around the kitchen opening cabinets and drawers. Cheap silverware in one drawer, pots and pans in a cabinet. In the refrigerator, bottles of condiments in the door racks, a dish of baking soda. Nothing else.

It was almost full dark now. She flicked a wall switch near the back door. A light on the side of the garage went on, illuminating the yard.

He slid the clip back into the automatic, worked the slide, and lowered the hammer. The sound reminded her of what they'd come here to do.

She felt light-headed suddenly, as if she were on a fast-moving elevator, the floor pressing up against the soles of her feet. She took steady breaths until it passed.

"You all right?" he said.

She nodded. There was a sour burning in her stomach. "Time to make that call."

When the phone in his pocket buzzed, Eddie was at a rest stop on Interstate 95, leaning against the hood of the Mercury. He took it out, looked at the number, pressed SEND, lifted it to his ear. Traffic blew by on the highway, past the sign that read WELCOME TO CONNECTICUT.

"I'm going to tell you where I am," the woman said. "You need to write it down?"

"No."

"Then listen carefully. I don't want you getting it wrong, getting lost up here."

"One thing at a time. You have what we talked about?"

A pause. "Yes."

"All of it?"

"All that's left. One hundred, like I said."

"Tell me where you are."

He listened to the directions. He'd brought a Connecticut road map, would trace the route when he got back in the car.

"You get all that?" she said.

"Yeah."

"It should take you about two hours. You coming from Jersey?"

He looked up at the sign. "Yes."

"You want to come over the GWB, get on I-87 North. If you don't, you'll get lost before you've started."

"All right," he said. He guessed the distance to where she was. An hour's drive at most.

"The house is set back from the road," she said. "Come up the driveway. There's a light on the garage. My car's parked inside. I'll be in the house. When I see you drive up, I'll come out to meet you."

He almost smiled at that.

"Right," he said. "You alone?"

"Yes."

"Good," he said and closed the phone.

"Think he'll go for it?" Chance said.

They were sitting at the table in semidarkness.

"He's suspicious," she said, "but the money's too much of a hook. He'll be here. Way I figure, if he's coming from Jersey, that means two and a half, three hours to get up here, find the place."

"What bothers me is we don't even know what he looks like."

"Whoever shows up, that's him."

"And you say he might have a partner, too."

"Nothing for it. We'll just have to deal."

"He's got to know it's a trap."

"He wants that money, and he's got no other way of finding it. He'll have to take the chance. If he doesn't, I might be in the wind and gone. He knows I won't go back to the apartment. Only way he finds out if I'm for real or not is by coming up here."

Chance took two pair of flexicuffs from his pocket. "I brought these," he said. "Just in case."

"Let's hope it doesn't get to that."

"Where are you going to leave the car when we're done?"

"There are some fire roads north of here, no houses

around. I'll go up one of them, park the car in the trees, wipe it clean. The cold will keep the smell down. If we're lucky, no one will find him for a few days. We'll both be long gone by then."

"You know," he said, "it's not that easy."

"What?"

"Killing a man."

"I didn't think it was," she said.

"Have you ever done it?"

"Never even came close. Never had to."

He looked out the window. "I read once they did a study of soldiers in World War II. They wanted to figure out why, in a firefight, so many rounds get let off, but so few people actually get hit. They found only twenty-five percent of GIs could actually point a rifle at another human being and pull the trigger, even if that person was shooting at them. It's against human nature."

"I believe that."

"That changed with Vietnam, more automatic weapons. Soldiers could spray and pray, and were still likely to hit someone, whether they were looking in his eyes or not. Technology depersonalized it."

"What's your point?"

"I was working outside Detroit once. Before I knew Wayne. It was an armored car thing. Guy running it was an ex-marine named Spencer. Out of his mind. I was young and stupid, didn't know any better."

"What happened?"

"Four-man deal. Spencer, some seventeen-year-old punk he was bringing up, me, and the inside man, one of the truck guards, named Logan. It went okay, no one got hurt. Pretty big haul and a good split. Then the Feds started putting pressure on the guards."

"They always do."

"Spencer got paranoid. Whether Logan told them anything or not, who knows. Anyway, Spencer got the four of us together at an abandoned auto plant in Hamtramck to talk about it. Spencer's punk knew what was coming. I didn't.

"So we're sitting around what used to be the plant manager's office, and Logan's playing it pretty cool. I mean, if he had ratted, would he have come there in a million years? The punk gets up to take a leak. When he comes back, he goes behind where Logan's sitting, picks up this piece of wood, like this big, hits him on the side of the head, knocks him out of the chair."

He turned the flexicuffs over in his hands, looked at them, then put them back in his pocket.

"Guy's dazed, but he's conscious, knows what's going on. They tie him to a chair with duct tape, and Spencer takes this gun out from under his coat, a Colt Python, big piece of iron. I can see it like it was yesterday. He shakes five shells out, leaves one in, spins the cylinder, hands the gun to me. I tell him no fucking way.

"Then he takes another gun out, a .45, points it at my head. He tells me to take the Python or he'll shoot me right there, and that Logan has a better chance than I do. I believed him."

"What did you do?"

"I took the gun. I was a kid myself. Twenty-two. Scared shitless. So I point the gun at Logan, maybe three feet between us. His eyes are Ping-Pong balls. Spencer's got the .45

to my head the whole time. So I close my eyes and pull the trigger. Empty chamber."

He took a breath, looked away. She waited for him to go on.

"Logan pissed himself right there. First time I'd ever seen someone do that. Then Spencer has the kid take the gun, spin the cylinder again. Logan's crying like a baby now, telling them he hadn't said shit to anyone, wouldn't. I guess he thought he still had a chance."

"What happened then?"

"The kid took his turn. Empty chamber. Spencer spun it again, handed it to me. Put the .45 right here." He touched his left temple.

"So I point the gun at Logan again, pull the trigger." He looked at her. "Chamber wasn't empty that time."

"That's rough. I'm sorry."

"Not as sorry as Logan was."

"What did you do after that?"

"Got the fuck out of Michigan as fast I could. Never went back. A few years later, I heard Spencer got brought down during a bank takeover in Kalamazoo. SWAT sniper. I would have shaken the cop's hand."

She said nothing.

"That's the only time I ever pulled a trigger on anyone in my life."

They looked out the window. The moon was over the trees, cold and white as bone. The vague sense of dread she'd felt since they'd found Hector now seemed to take shape, like a presence in the room. She thought about Chance's story. Wondered if, when the time came, she could look into Eddie Santiago's eyes, pull the trigger.

"When this is done," Chance said, "I'm just going to head out of here, keep going west. What about you?"

"I've got things back at a hotel in the city. I'll pick up some more clothes from my apartment, get some cash together, stay on the down low for a while. Maybe head south, tend to some things."

He got up, went to the back door, looked out the porch windows.

"I was thinking I could set up in the garage," he said.

"No good. If he comes up that driveway, it'll be the first place he sees. He'll check it out. We don't want him running. We need to get him in the house."

"This guy's pretty smart, isn't he?"

"Smart enough, catch Hector the way he did."

"Or just lucky."

"Well, then," she said, "let's hope his luck's run out."

THIRTY

The house was easy to find. Eddie drove past, saw the mailbox, the number. A light on the garage, like she'd said. Fresh tire tracks running up the driveway. Nothing but woods around it.

The next house was a half mile down on the same side, no lights on and no cars in the driveway. He came to an intersection with a blinking yellow signal, made a right, the road taking him deeper into the woods. At another intersection, he turned again. No houses back here. He looked at the odometer, estimating the distance, slowed. He would be somewhere behind the house now. Far off through the trees, he saw the glow of the garage light.

He nosed the Mercury into a stand of fir trees, cut the lights and engine. He waited there, the window down, listening to the engine tick as it cooled. No other sounds. He got out of the car, popped the trunk.

The shotgun was cold through the gloves. He took extra

shells from the bag. The Star was in his right-hand pocket, the Ruger in his left. He touched his pants pocket to make sure the razor was there, shut the trunk, locked the car with the keypad. He looked off into the trees. The garage light would make a good landmark, keep him from getting lost.

The shotgun at his side, he headed into the woods.

Crissa popped the cylinder of the .38, rotated it to check the rounds again.

"How many times you going to do that?" Chance said. He was standing by the kitchen window, looking out.

"Sorry. Nervous habit." She locked the cylinder back into place. The burning in her stomach was worse.

"I was thinking," he said. "We should have something on the floor. Is there a shower curtain upstairs?"

"No good. When we clean up afterward, I want to leave this place the way we found it. We'll have to take our chances."

"I saw a blanket out in the garage. If it's heavy enough, we could use it to carry him, then leave it in the trunk with him."

"Okay."

He tucked the automatic into his belt, the jacket covering it.

On the porch, he looked back at her. "Hey, Red?"

"Yeah?"

"If this goes bad . . ."

She waited.

"Never mind," he said.

Eddie made his way through the trees, keeping the light in front of him. He could see the house now, a faint glow in one window. The woods had thinned, so he went slower, watching his footing, feet already numb from the cold.

He came out of the woods behind the garage, staying away from the light. He looked in a side window, saw the car inside, a screwdriver wedged into the ignition, wires hanging from the steering column.

With his back to the wall, he looked around the corner of the garage. A man came out of the porch and into the yard, stepping carefully. He was trying to follow a trail already there. So there were at least two of them inside.

The man crossed the yard, headed toward the garage. Eddie raised the shotgun.

The burning in her stomach had become a stabbing pain. She could taste the lunch she'd had hours ago. When Chance left, she went upstairs to the windowless bathroom, closed the door, turned on the light.

Another spasm in her stomach, and then she was kneeling in front of the toilet, gagging. She vomited twice, mostly fluid, then dry-heaved until the spasms stopped. Her face was wet with sweat.

She drank water from the faucet, spit, drank more. Then she flushed the toilet, took a hand towel from a shelf, wiped everything down again. Get yourself together, she thought. Work the plan.

When the man was almost at the garage, Eddie came around the corner and aimed the shotgun at his chest. "Stop."

The man squinted, trying to see past the garage light. Eddie came forward, his finger tightening on the trigger. The man took a step back.

"Whoah," he said.

"Are you Chance?"

"Who are you?" His hands were in view, but he kept taking slow steps back, trying to put distance between them.

"Yeah, I guess you are," Eddie said. "She in there?"

"Who?" Chance said.

"She bring my money?"

Chance raised his hands, still backing away. "I think maybe you got the wrong place."

"Call her. Get her out here."

"I'm going to turn around now, and walk back to my house."

"Your house, huh?"

"And then I'm going to call the police."

"Go ahead."

Chance took two more backward steps, then turned, started toward the house. Eddie let him go, knew what was coming.

Halfway to the house, Chance turned fast, a gun in his hand. He aimed, twisting like a duelist to offer less of a target.

Eddie fired. It blew Chance off his feet, dropped him facedown in the snow, the gun flying away. Eddie worked the pump, the spent shell flying out, waited for him to move again.

She jumped when she heard the blast, grabbed the .38. In the back bedroom, she looked out on the yard, saw Chance on the ground, motionless. There was a man standing beside the garage with a shotgun.

She fired, blew out the center of the window, then fired again through the hole she'd made. Snow kicked up near the man's feet. He looked up at her, raised the shotgun.

Eddie saw the woman at the window, the muzzle flashes, heard the pop of a round passing close by. He fired just as she backed away. Buckshot took out the rest of the glass, billowed the curtains. He pumped, fired again, shredding the window frame. Wood splinters and glass fell onto the porch roof.

Chance was moving, crawling toward the house, the snow turning red beneath him. Eddie pointed the shotgun at him, then let the barrel drop. He walked over, planted a foot on Chance's back to hold him there, touched the muzzle to the back of his head.

Eddie looked back at the house, the second-floor window.

"Two ways this ends," he called out. "You decide which."

She sat on the floor, back to the wall, cold wind coming through the shattered window above her. She opened the .38, pulled the spent shells out, thumbed new ones in, fumbling with gloved fingers.

Glass crunched under her feet as she stood, moved away from the window. Santiago called up to her.

"You know what I came here for. That's all I want."

She went downstairs and into the kitchen, moved to the window. She got her first clear look at him in the garage light. A big man in a trench coat and sweater. He had a foot on Chance's back, a pistol-grip shotgun to his head. He leaned forward, and Chance groaned.

"He'll live. Long as no one gets stupid. You want him, come get him. But you need to toss that gun out here first."

When she didn't answer, he said, "He's going to bleed out here soon, that what you want? You get him inside, you might be able to do something for him."

She went out onto the porch, staying low in the shadows.

"You need to come out here," he said. "But throw that piece first. This thing's got a hair trigger. You take another potshot at me—or anyone else comes out of that house with you—and he'll get it first, then you."

"There's no one else."

"All right, then. Come on out."

She pushed the porch door open, stood at an angle to it.

"Right there's good," he said. "Lose the gun."

She tossed the .38 into the snow.

"Okay," he said. "Come get him."

He stepped away, watching her. She went to Chance, knelt. He was breathing shallowly, his eyes closed. She got an arm under his, tried to lift him out of the bloody snow. He gasped. She set him back down, opened his jacket. On his upper right side and shoulder, the sweater was torn and black with blood.

"Get him up."

"Bobby," she said into his ear. "We need to get you inside."
He half-opened his eyes.

"Come on," she said. "You'll be all right."

She switched sides, away from the wounds, got his arm around her shoulder. She stood slowly, taking his weight. He moaned, gripped her tighter, finally straightening his legs.

"There you go," she said.

When he had his feet under him, she began to walk him toward the door.

Santiago bent and picked up her .38, pocketed it.

"In the house," he said.

Chance was fading in and out, but still walking. Santiago followed them in.

"The kitchen," he said. "Right there on the floor is good."

She got him through the door just in time, his legs going loose again. She eased him to the floor. Her gloves were slick with blood, a dark smear of it down her coat.

"Turn around," Santiago said. "Let me get a look at you."

When she did, the butt of the shotgun came at her in a blur. It thumped into the side of her head, and suddenly she was facedown on the floor.

"Stay there," he said.

The room seemed to spin around her, and she felt a surge of nausea. She saw him set the shotgun on the floor, go through Chance's pockets. He took out the two pair of flexicuffs, looked over at her. "These for me?"

Chance groaned.

"You stay right there," Santiago told him. He picked up the shotgun, came back to her. She was seeing double from her left eye. The warm muzzle touched the side of her face.

He put a knee in her back, pinned her there, patted her down. He took away her pick set and pocketknife, left the loose shells.

"Anything else on you I should know about?"

When he set the shotgun down, she bucked hard against him, trying to throw him off. He put a forearm across her throat, pulled back until she couldn't breathe. "Don't fight me."

She felt her arms being pulled behind her, plastic cinching around her wrists. This is it, she thought. You lost your chance. He's going to kill both of you.

She looked over at Chance. He lay facedown, not moving. Blood was spreading slowly across the floor.

Santiago stood, kicked her left ankle. She drew it in reflexively and he knelt on her calf, brought her feet together, bound her ankles with the other pair of cuffs. She heard the ratcheting as he drew them tight.

He moved around in front of her, squatted, showed her the shotgun. "You know who this belonged to?"

She watched him, the double vision lesser now.

"Your friend Hector. I took it off him."

From a pants pocket, he drew out a straight razor with a bone handle.

"And this, I got off your buddy Stimmer." He opened the blade. "I used it on Hector for a while. I can use it on you, too."

He held the blade in front of her face. "The money."

Time, she thought. You've got to buy time. She breathed deep, looked at him. He tapped the flat of the blade against her cheek. She winced, closed her eyes.

"Look at me. Or I'll take those eyelids off."

She opened her eyes.

"The money," he said again. "It's here, right?"

She nodded.

"Where?"

"In the car."

"The one in the garage?"

"Yes. In the trunk."

"Good girl." He stood, folded the razor, put it away, picked up the shotgun.

"Don't go anywhere," he said. "I'll be back."

He walked through snow to the garage. He set the shotgun on the car roof, opened the driver's door, got in, looked at the ignition. It was a professional job, the screwdriver as good as a key now. When he was done here, he'd take the car, drive it back to where the Mercury was parked, save himself another trip through the woods.

He looked in the glove box, felt under the seats, then pulled the trunk latch.

Rolling onto her back was easy. The double vision in her left eye had faded to a faint blurriness. She crabbed across the floor, got her back against the refrigerator. Chance lay silent.

The floor was wet from the snow they'd tracked in. She pushed with both feet, locked her legs, her boots scrabbling for traction. The refrigerator swayed back, something clanging inside. She pushed harder, until her back began to slide up the front of the door. In a few seconds, she was standing.

She shuffled her feet toward the stove, her fingers finding a burner knob. She pushed, twisted it all the way.

Looking back over her shoulder, she saw the right front burner start to glow. Slowly, it went from a dull red to a deeper orange. A wisp of smoke came off it, from dust and disuse.

She clenched her fists. The gloves would give some protection, but not for long. More than anything, she would have to keep her balance. If she fell, it was all over.

The heating coil was bright now, and she could feel its warmth. She stretched her arms as far back as they would go, held her breath, and pushed her wrists into the burner.

He opened the overnight bag, saw the money inside, dumped it out into the trunk. Banded stacks; fifties, hundreds. He pushed them around. Ten grand at most.

"Lying bitch."

He pulled back the trunk carpet, looked in the wheel well, beneath the spare. Nothing.

He could use the razor on the woman, get her to tell him where the rest was—if there was any. But then he would have to figure out how to get it, start all this over again, only this time alone. It wasn't worth it. Better to take what was here, cut his losses, go back in and kill them both.

She could smell burning plastic now, the stink of smoldering leather. Smoke drifted up behind her, the burner scorching her right hand through the glove. She shifted to get a better angle, cried out as bare skin touched the heating element. Pain rushed up her right arm, watered her eyes.

She pulled her hands away from the burner, could smell her own flesh burning. She'd seen a paring knife in the silverware drawer. If she could get through the wrist cuffs, she could use it to cut through the ones on her ankles. It wouldn't be much of a weapon, but it would have to do. She had no other chance.

She looked behind her, trying to center the cuffs on the edge of the burner. She bit into her lip, tasted blood, and pushed down hard.

He put the money back in the bag, zipped it up. It would have to do.

He shut the trunk, got the shotgun from the roof. When he left the garage, he used the butt to break the light fixture on the wall. The yard went dark.

The snow around him seemed to glow in the moonlight. He walked back to the house.

THIRTY-ONE

As soon as he entered the porch, he smelled it, the acrid stench of burned plastic and leather. He shouldered through the kitchen door, came in with the shotgun up, finger on the trigger.

Chance was gone, just a puddle of blood on the floor there now. Eddie swung the shotgun toward where he'd left the woman. He saw the orange glow of the burner, the smoking gloves on the floor, and then she was coming out of the shadows, a knife in her hand.

Crissa went for his face, jabbing with the paring knife, trying for the eyes. He got the shotgun up, blocked it, and her next thrust went through his right coat sleeve and deep into his upper arm.

He grunted, swung the shotgun at her, and she grabbed it with both hands, tried to twist it out of his grip, couldn't. He spun her, drove her back, and she felt the refrigerator rock as she hit it. But she had a solid grip on the gun now, wouldn't let go.

His lips pulled back, and she could see his teeth, smell his breath. He was trying to get the shotgun across her throat, the knife still dangling from his arm. She let him get in close, then used her knees, jacking them up into his thighs, trying for the groin. He twisted away to protect himself, his grip on the gun loosening, and that was all she needed.

She pulled him to her, drove the top of her head into his face, and then he was falling back, sliding in Chance's blood, and she had the shotgun.

He came up faster than she expected, getting his footing, drawing her .38. She swung the shotgun. The stock cracked into his wrist, and the .38 flew away, hit the wall. She turned the muzzle toward him, and he was diving for the porch, throwing himself into the blackness as she squeezed the trigger.

He heard the blast as he hit the floor. The center porch window exploded and collapsed. He rolled away, heard her pump and fire again, buckshot shredding the floor where he'd been. He got to his feet, lunged for the porch door, hit it, and tumbled out into the snow. The window above his head detonated, blew glass over him. He ran into the darkness.

She tracked him through the shattered windows, the shotgun up, glass at her feet. The garage light was out, the yard lit only by the moon. She saw the solidity of his shadow, fired, the gun kicking back hard. She worked the pump again, the smoking shell flying to her right. The breech closed with a hollow click. Empty.

She went back into the kitchen, tossed the shotgun on the counter, picked up the .38. Her hands stung. She shut off the stove light, ducked below the level of the kitchen windows, listened. The only sound was the wind.

Staying low, she moved into the dining room. Chance lay where she had dragged him.

She knelt beside him. He opened his eyes.

"Hey," she said. "You're back."

He shifted, winced.

"Don't move." She set the .38 down, opened his jacket.

"He got me good," he said. His voice was weak.

"Yeah, he did." She gently pulled the sweater away from his wounds. He gasped as she ripped the material along the pellet holes, exposing his chest and shoulder. The wounds were clustered high, all of them steadily oozing blood.

"A little lower and that would have been it," she said. "But what you caught doesn't look too deep. Can you move your right arm?"

"A little."

"Good."

"Where is he?"

"Out there somewhere."

"You hit him?"

"I don't think so."

"Too bad."

"Don't move. I'll be back."

She picked up the .38, went upstairs. Wind blew down the hall from the broken back window. She crouched beside it, looked out on the moonlit snow. There was a maze of tracks from the three of them. She couldn't tell which were his.

In the bathroom, she closed the door tight, turned the light on, set the gun on the sink. Her hands were throbbing, both wrists bright red and spotted with pale blisters. She ran water over them, the pain shooting up into her shoulders. After a few moments, the burning began to subside.

In the medicine cabinet, she found rubbing alcohol and a box of large gauze pads. She took a clean hand towel from the shelf, then turned the light off, opened the door to listen. He might not run, she knew. He might just double back, try to find a way into the house.

She carried everything downstairs. Chance had worked himself into a sitting position against the wall.

"I told you not to move," she said. She knelt, set the .38 on the floor.

"I don't want to pass out again."

"You may anyway. This is going to hurt." She pulled the ragged edges of the sweater wider, uncapped the alcohol, looked in his eyes. "Easy now."

She poured alcohol down his shoulder and chest, washing through the clotting blood. He cried out, stiffened, closed his eyes. The pungent smell of it drifted up.

"You still with me?" she said.

He nodded, opened his eyes. She shook three gauze pads from the box, tore them open. She laid them on his chest and shoulder, covering most of the pellet wounds. Almost immediately, the gauze began to darken.

She folded the hand towel, placed it on his chest. "Hold this against yourself. Keep up the pressure."

She guided his left hand to the towel, helped him hold it there. He winced again.

She sat back on her haunches. "We have to get you to a hospital."

He looked up at her. "You think he's still out there?"

"Yes."

"What are you going to do?"

She picked up the .38.

"Go find him," she said.

THIRTY-TWO

She went out the front door. The wind had stopped. She listened, then cocked the .38 as quietly as she could. Rounding the corner of the house, she looked up the driveway. Moonlight gleamed on the snow.

She started toward the rear of the house, staying close to the wall. When she reached the back porch she stopped and looked out into the stillness of the yard. The snow began to darken. Clouds moved in front of the moon.

The garage was a darker shape ahead. He might be inside there, waiting for her to show herself. Or anywhere in the trees, with another weapon, waiting for a clear shot.

She raised the .38 in a two-handed grip, pointed it into the yard, searching for a silhouette, a shadow. Hoping she'd be quicker on the trigger than he was.

She started toward the garage. The clouds parted again, bathed the ground in moonlight. A gleam in the driveway caught her eye, right on the edge of the woods. Something metallic there in the snow. She moved closer. It was the paring knife, the blade shiny with blood. So he'd gone that way, back into the trees. He'd have a car out there somewhere, on the other side.

She was in the center of the driveway when she heard the click of the Toyota's ignition, the roar of its engine. She turned toward the garage just as the car came skidding and screeching out of it, aiming at her. She twisted to run toward the house. Knew she wouldn't make it.

Eddie looked over his shoulder, steered at her, heard the fleshy thump as he caught her with the left rear fender. Halfway down the driveway, he hit the brakes hard, and the Toyota slewed to a stop, pointing toward the house.

He turned on the headlights, saw the woman in their glare, struggling to stand. It had only been a glancing blow, not solid enough to put her down for good. She was on her feet now, dragging one leg. She looked down the driveway at him, blinded by his lights.

He slammed the gearshift into DRIVE, pressed the gas pedal to the floor.

She heard the Toyota's engine, the buzz saw whine of its tires fighting for traction. In the blaze of the headlights, she saw the .38 a few feet away, lying in the snow.

She dragged her right leg, bent for the gun. She heard the tires grip and squeal, and then the car was coming at her, and she had the gun, was turning with it, into the lights. Aim, she thought. Make it count. Even if he kills you.

She fired at a spot above the headlights, the gun jumping in her hand, fired again, and then the car was veering toward the house. She threw herself to the left, the front fender missing her by inches, and landed hard on the frozen ground.

When the first shot came through the windshield, Eddie turned his face away, the glass spraying across him. He aimed the car at her, standing there in his headlights, and the next shot starred the windshield above the steering wheel, scored his neck. He twisted the wheel to the left, and then the woman was moving to the side, out of the way, and he slammed hard on the brakes, but it was too late. The house filled his vision.

The Toyota hit the house just under the dining room windows, the front end punching into the siding, then bouncing back with the impact. She saw the driver's side air bag bloom open.

The engine was still running. It steadily pushed the car's crumpled front end back into the wall again. Steam hissed out from under the wrecked hood, then a puff of darker smoke.

When she got up, her right leg and hip were numb. She opened the .38, picked out the empty shells, reloaded. Moving to the center of the driveway, she raised the gun, the car about fifteen feet away.

The whine of the engine grew louder, higher, and then there was a burst of black smoke from beneath the hood. Flames began to dart out from around its edges, blistering the paint. The engine coughed and died. Ruptured fuel line, she thought, spilling gasoline onto the hot manifold.

The air bag had deflated. Santiago was slumped motionless over the wheel. Her only angle on him was through the passenger side windows. She steadied the .38, centered the front sight on his silhouette.

But she couldn't squeeze the trigger.

The heat woke him. He opened his eyes, and the loose air bag was in his lap, the gunpowder smell of it in the air. He was powdered with white dust. Faint steam rose from the floor.

He touched his forehead, felt blood there, his hand a blur. There were two wide holes in the windshield, the glass spiderwebbed around them. More blood on his neck, the shoulder of his trench coat.

He could see flames coming from under the hood. They were running up the wall of the house, blackening the siding.

He yanked on the door handle, pushed. It groaned, held. The impact had jammed it. He butted it again, felt it give slightly. Smoke began to filter through the dashboard vents. He could hear the crackle of the flames now, the windshield darkening.

The third time he hit the door, it popped open, stiff and creaking. He slid out, fell into water, the heat from the fire melting the snow. Thick black smoke was filling the car now. The air stank of burning plastic and rubber.

He crawled through the slush, staying low, knowing the woman was somewhere on the other side. He leaned against the left rear fender, the metal warm against his back, got the guns out. He cocked the Ruger, then the Star, had a sudden memory of finding it in Casco's safe, taking his money. The day he'd gotten out. The day it had all started.

Steam rose off the ground around him. The fire would reach the gas tank soon. He had to get up, find the woman, end it.

The wind was back up, blowing the smoke in her direction. She moved away, her eyes watering. Her right leg had no strength, but the numbness had turned to pain, and that was good.

She'd heard the creak of the door opening, had seen Santiago slip out of sight. Now smoke all but obscured the car, and she couldn't tell where he'd gone.

Flames were climbing the wall. The dining room windows had shattered from the impact, and the curtains were on fire. She thought of Chance inside.

She pointed the .38 into the wall of smoke and waited.

Eddie stood. He held the Star in his right hand, the Ruger in his left. He drew in breath, tried to remember where he'd last seen the woman. Farther up the driveway, if she was still there, if she hadn't fled into the woods or back to the house.

Time to get it over with, he thought.

He wheeled around the back of the burning car, came

through the smoke, guns up, and there she was, in the driveway, closer than he'd expected, feet spread apart, .38 in a two-handed grip. He started to squeeze both triggers, and suddenly he was stumbling back, his breath gone. He went down hard, the ground tilting under him, saw trees, clouds, the moon.

The bitch shot me, he thought. She shot me bad.

Crissa watched him go down, the sound of the shot echoing in her ears. The round had hit him in the left side of the chest, driven him back. She thought about the cross-etched bullet, the damage it would do.

He rolled from his back to his side. She cocked the .38 again. Slowly, he made it to his knees. He'd lost one gun. Now he raised the other, let it drop for a moment, turned his head, and spit blood on the ground. Then he seemed to look past her, at something in the trees.

She settled the sight on his chest. There was a faint tremble in her hands. Please don't make me do it, she thought. Just toss the gun away, and we'll leave. The money's not worth it. Nothing's worth it.

He smiled and there was blood in his teeth. He met her eyes, raised the gun again.

Eddie coughed hard. There was blood in it, the coppery taste strong. He lifted the Star, then lowered it. It weighed too much.

His eyes were blurry from the smoke. He spit, looked at the woman, trying to focus. There was someone in the trees behind her. As he watched, the figure took shape in the moonlight. It was Terry. He'd been there all along, watching them. Eddie blinked, squinted, and then there was nothing in the trees but darkness.

He looked back at the woman, aimed the Star at her, began to squeeze the trigger.

He never felt the bullet.

THIRTY-THREE

The house was full of smoke. Chance had dragged himself into the kitchen, was crawling toward the porch. Behind him, flames were licking up the dining room wall.

She caught his left arm, lifted, got it around her neck, stood with him. He leaned against her, and they made their way onto the porch, then into the yard. She set him down in the snow, looked back at the house. Flames had reached the roof, were crawling under the eaves, smoke pouring out.

"Where is he?" Chance said.

"Dead. Come on." She got him to his feet again, walked him through the snow toward the woods. His legs were unsteady, but they stayed under him. She had her right arm tight around his waist, her left bracing his wrist across her shoulder.

"Where we going?" he said.

"Try to find his car."

Ashes and soot drifted down on them. She could hear sirens far away.

"Come on," she said. "You can make it."

The Toyota's gas tank went up with a flat boom. The trunk yawned open, flames billowing out. A glowing ember twirled through the air, landed in the snow in front of her. It was half of a twenty-dollar bill.

They were into the trees now. She stopped, looked back. The roof was on fire, a mammoth cloud of smoke filling the sky, blotting out the moon.

The sirens were louder, closer.

"Red . . . we need to get out of here."

"I know."

"Now."

There was a loud *crack,* and a section of roof caved in, sparks swirling up. She watched them rise into the sky.

"Red . . ."

"Yeah," she said. "Let's go."

She turned her back on the house.

After a while, they reached a road, stumbled along it until she saw the car parked in the trees.

"There it is," she said.

"I need to sit."

She lowered him to the snowy ground. Her right leg was stiff, her hip aching.

The Mercury was locked. She looked around, found a heavy stone stuck in the frost. She got it loose, lifted it over her head, and smashed it into the passenger side window until the glass gave way.

She dropped the stone, reached in and unlocked the door, brushed glass from the seat. She helped him up, got him into the car. He leaned over, popped the driver's side lock.

She slid behind the wheel, realized then she had no tools. No pocketknife, no pick set. She clawed at the plastic on the steering column, the pain in her wrists flaring. No good.

"Son of a *bitch*," she said. She got back out, held on to the door and roof for support, heel-kicked the steering column until the plate broke. Back behind the wheel, she pulled the plastic loose, tugged at the wires.

"Can you do it?" he said.

"Shut up and let me concentrate."

It took her three tries. Relief flooded through her when the wires sparked and the engine turned over. She backed out onto the road, swung around to head south, lights off.

Cold air filled the car as she drove. They came to a four-way stop sign, and an ambulance blew across their path, lights flashing, siren rising and falling.

The clouds had parted, and the moon was out again. With the headlights off, she wound her way back to where they'd left the Mustang. It was alone in the lot. Through the trees, she could see a parade of emergency lights on a parallel road. In the distance, the sky glowed red.

When she pulled up alongside the Mustang, Chance's eyes were closed. She pulled wires loose to kill the engine.

"Hey," she said. He didn't move.

She touched his shoulder, and his eyes snapped open. His face was slick with sweat.

"Your keys."

He looked at her, confused.

"Give me your car keys."

He nodded, reached slowly into a pocket, drew out two keys on a ring. She took them.

"Leave me," he said.

"I can't do that."

"You have to."

"No, I don't."

She got out, opened the Mustang's passenger door, came back. His eyes were closed again, his chin on his chest. When she opened the door, he slumped out. She caught him before he hit the ground.

"Come on," she said. "Work with me."

She pulled his arm over her shoulder, helped him get his feet under him.

"Leave me," he said.

"Quiet."

She walked him around the Mustang, got him into the seat, shut the door.

She needed something to wipe the Mercury down. They'd left evidence back at the house, but there was nothing she could do about that now. The car was different.

She popped the Mercury's trunk, looking for a rag. Inside were an olive drab duffel and an oversized gym bag. There were clothes in the duffel. She pulled out a T-shirt, saw white plastic below it. Her laptop. She drew it out. Beneath it were banded stacks of money.

She looked at them for a moment, then dumped them into the trunk. Twenties and fifties.

She filled the gym bag with money, put the laptop in, zipped it up, and slung it over her shoulder. She shut the trunk, used the wadded-up T-shirt to wipe down everything she might have touched.

The gym bag went into the Mustang's trunk. When she got behind the wheel, Chance was out again. She started the engine, backed out, and headed south once more, away from the sirens and the glow in the sky.

Ten minutes later, she saw the first yellow hospital sign. She followed them into a small downtown, all the stores dark. The hospital was an island of light at the end of the street. Big glass doors and a red neon sign that said EMERGENCY.

She pulled to the curb, killed the headlights. They were three blocks from the hospital, but even from here she could see the security cameras over the doors.

Chance opened his eyes. "Where are we?"

She pointed at the hospital. "This is as far as I can take you."

He nodded. "All right."

"I'm sorry."

He looked at her, pulled his coat tighter around himself. "Don't be, Red."

He opened his door, paused as if gathering strength. She put a hand on his forearm, squeezed. He gave her a slack smile.

"Go on," he said. "Get out of here while you can."

He pulled himself out of the car, leaned on the roof, looked in at her.

"See you when I see you," he said and shut the door.

She watched him walk away, leaning against parked cars and meters for support. When he reached the emergency room, he stepped into the lights, sank to his knees, triggered the automatic doors. He rolled onto his side, and two white-coated EMTs rushed out.

Headlights still off, she U-turned in the street, drove away.

It had started to snow again, hard and icy, clicking as it hit the car. After a half hour behind the wheel, her eyes were closing, her limbs heavy. She pulled into a Quality Inn outside Oxford, used the T-shirt to wipe the blood from her jacket and the car seat.

She checked in using her Roberta Summersfield ID. It took all she had to carry the gym bag up to the second-floor room. She hung the DO NOT DISTURB tag, set the night latch, turned the heat up.

Her clothes smelled of smoke. She peeled them off, ran the shower. Her right leg was bruised from hip to knee, a deep blotch of yellow and purple. On her left wrist, the skin around her tattoo was swollen and blistered.

She stood under the hot spray for a long time, her eyes closing, only the pain in her wrists and leg keeping her awake. Afterward, she wrapped herself in a towel, unzipped the gym bag, spilled its contents out on the bed. It took her ten minutes to count it all. She kept losing track, having to start again. It came out to forty thousand and change.

She powered up the laptop, checked the folder. Maddie's pictures were still there. She looked through them all twice.

The low-battery light began to blink in a corner of the screen.

She shut the laptop off, put all the money back in the bag. Then she lay back on the bed, looked up at the ceiling.

Suddenly she was cold, shaking. She sat up, wrapped the covers around herself, but couldn't stop trembling. She began to rock back and forth, eyes closed tight against the tears that were spilling out.

The last thing she did before sleep was get the .38 from her jacket, check the door again. She slid the gun under a pillow, turned out all the lights but one, crawled naked between the sheets. She fell asleep listening to the wind.

THIRTY-FOUR

She woke at eleven, groggy and stiff, hard sunlight pouring through the gap in the curtains. She showered again, the steam rising around her. Every muscle ached.

Her clothes still smelled of smoke. She got them back on, her leg throbbing, put the .38 in the gym bag, and limped out to the Mustang. The day was bright and clear, the air sharp.

She found a Walgreens nearby, bought gauze, tape, burn cream, and Tylenol. Back in the car, she smeared cream on her wrists, taped gauze over it. Soon, the pain began to lessen.

When she got back on 95, she tuned in WCBS Newsradio, but there was nothing about Chance or the fire. She stopped for breakfast, washed down four Tylenol with two cups of tea, then got on the road again.

When she saw signs for New York City, she pulled off the highway, drove until buildings and houses gave way to fields and woods. After a while, she saw what she wanted, the glint of sunlit water through the trees.

She followed a road that led to a stone bridge over a river, no other cars around, no houses nearby. She pulled over, opened the trunk, got out the .38.

The current was running fast, gathering speed beneath the bridge. She dumped the last of the loose shells into the water, then opened the .38 and shook out the spent casings.

She looked at the gun, turned it over in her hand, remembering the day Wayne had given it to her. A long time ago.

She tossed the gun out over the river, watched it fall, splash, and disappear.

Back in the city, she went to the Travel Inn, changed clothes, and transferred all the money to her suitcase. She'd drop it at the apartment, call Rathka. The sooner she turned it over, the better she'd feel.

She checked out, bought a new cell from a corner deli, got the Mustang from the garage, and headed north on the West Side Highway. She got off on West 96th, took Broadway up to 108th, turned right.

There was a police cruiser in the loading zone outside her building. Behind it was an unmarked Crown Victoria with a whip antenna, blackwalls. Detectives.

She slowed, powered the window down halfway. Through the foyer door, she could see two uniforms in the lobby, talking to Reynaldo the doorman. That meant the detectives were already upstairs.

She heard a noise, saw the cat with the torn ear leap from

the stoop to the sidewalk. It sat beside a planter, looked across at her, totally still.

"Sorry," Crissa said.

A horn sounded behind her. There was a cab in her rear-view. She was blocking the street.

She powered the window up. The cat watched her as she drove away.

Circling back to 101st, she found a parking space near the bank. She got the new cell from its package, activated it, called Rathka's office.

It rang a long time. Rathka answered with a simple "Hello?"

"Why are you answering the phone?" she said. "Where's Monique?"

There was a pause, then, "Ah, Miss Anderson, I thought you might call. Monique's busy at the moment, helping out some unexpected visitors."

"Who's there?" she said.

"Sorry I can't stay on the line. Maybe you can try me later in the week?"

Voices in the background, muffled.

"Police?" she said.

"Yes, that's right. Thursday or Friday would be best."

Close by him, an unfriendly voice said, "Who is that?"

"Thanks," she told him and ended the call.

She took the cell apart in her lap. It was no good now. The number would be in Rathka's phone. She snapped the circuit board in half, tossed the pieces out the window.

They'd worked fast. Talked to the realty office in Connecticut, came up with the name Roberta Summersfield, backtracked to Rathka and the apartment. So the name was no good anymore. If they looked into it, they'd hit a dead end, but it might only whet their interest, keep them looking. Her life here was done.

She watched the front of the bank, wondering if they'd gotten that far, if there were police inside. She'd have to take the chance. She got out the ring of safe deposit keys.

Ten minutes later, she walked out of the bank with ten thousand dollars in banded fifties, a .32 automatic, and a U.S. passport and New Jersey driver's license in the name of Linda Hendryx. She drove around to two more Manhattan banks and did the same. When she was done, she had thirty-five thousand in cash. She put it in the suitcase with the rest of the money.

It took forever to get through the Lincoln Tunnel. She watched the rearview the entire time, waiting to see police lights. When the traffic finally broke up on the other side, she followed signs to the New Jersey Turnpike, headed south.

She'd drive as long as she could stay awake, get as far from the city as possible. Maybe west then, cross-country to the Coast, somewhere warm, or back up to Pennsylvania eventually, see if Charlie Glass could put together some work, get her going again. Money for Maddie, money for Wayne.

Eventually she'd call Rathka from somewhere far away, find out how much damage had been done, where things stood in Texas. Somehow she'd figure it all out, make it work.

It was growing dark, the sky clear. Stars were coming out,

flickers of cold and distant light. Nothing behind her now. Nothing but night ahead. But she had a name, a suitcase full of cash, a car, and a gun.

It was a start.